MARRIED BY FATE

AN ARRANGED MARRIAGES OF THE FAE NOVEL

BY JENNY HICKMAN

TEARMANN SEA
TEARMANN
THE BLACK FOREST
AIRREN
AIRREN SEA
N
NW
NE
W
E
SW
SE
S
FAE LANDS
IODALE
VELLAN

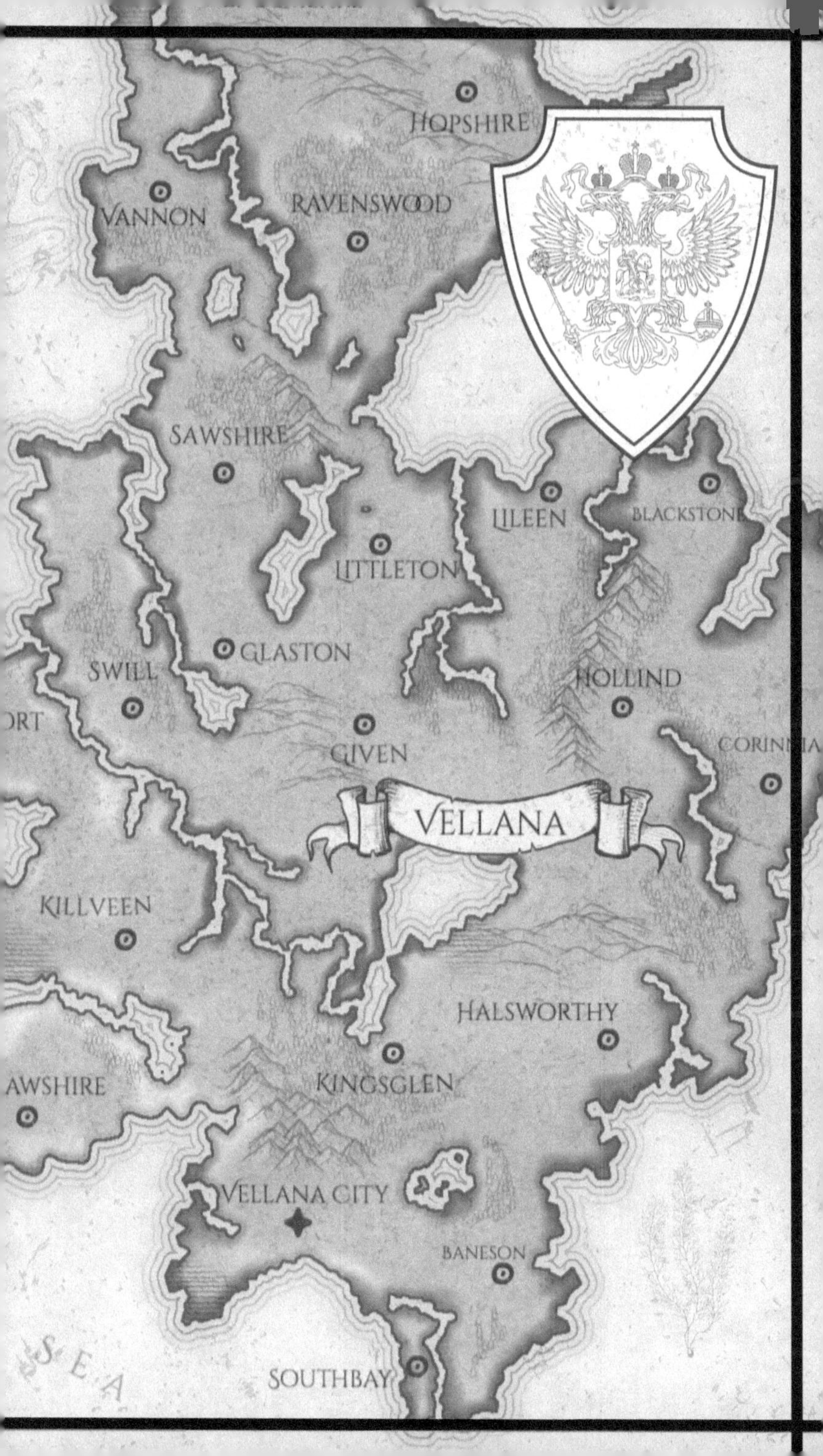

HOPSHIRE
VANNON
RAVENSWOOD
SAWSHIRE
LILEEN
BLACKSTONE
LITTLETON
GLASTON
SWILL
HOLLIND
CORINNA
ORT
GIVEN
VELLANA
KILLVEEN
HALSWORTHY
AWSHIRE
KINGSGLEN
VELLANA CITY
BANESON
SEA
SOUTHBAY

For my nieces Emma and Avery.

*Since this is probably the first book of mine
that your mother will let you read.*

PROLOGUE

It wasn't love at first sight.

Yet she believed from the moment she chose him that she'd found her life's purpose.

The young prince had broad shoulders, golden hair that caught the flickering candlelight, and eyes bluer than the skies in Iodale. His smile exuded confidence. His stance exuded power.

She'd been terrified when her parents had said she would be betrothed to a human prince. Fourteen was too young for a fae to even begin contemplating marriage, yet the moment she set foot in the castle's red and gold throne room, it was all she could think of.

Suddenly, the four years she would have to wait to become his bride felt like a lifetime.

Prince Alrec of Vellana.

His name became a treasure more valuable than any she owned.

Lady Roisin Newland would learn to love Prince Alrec, first son of King Bedwyr of Vellana.

And she could not wait to be queen.

It was love at first sight.

He had known from the moment his eyes connected with hers that he'd never love another.

She was tall and slim, with deeply tanned skin that glowed as if she'd swallowed the sun, and hair the color of freshly fallen snow.

He thought he'd known what to expect from a fae. He'd combed the library for books about them, studied the legends of their magic and beauty. But all the research in the world couldn't have prepared him for the sight of her.

Fifteen was too young to think of marriage. Suddenly, the four years he'd have to wait for her to move to the castle felt like a lifetime.

Lady Roisin Newland.

Her name was a song, more melodic than any he'd heard.

Prince Caiman, second son of King Bedwyr of Vellana, loved Lady Roisin Newland.

And he dreaded the day she would become his brother's wife.

1

―――――

ROISIN

LOVE'S MADNESS HAD CONSUMED ME FOR FOUR TEDIOUS years.

I kept expecting the obsession to wane but every morning I woke it grew stronger, as if fed by the stars and moon. And now that my mother and I had relocated to the castle in Vellana, the wait for my wedding day had become as unbearable as the summer sun beating down on my brow.

Streams of water spurted from the mouths of six golden lions, splashing into a deep pool of lily pads and orange fish. The scent of rose petals and stagnant water clung to the humid air. With my bare toes sinking deeper into the soft grass, I dipped my fingers into the pond, watching more ripples spread across the surface. If I kept still, the fish would grow used to my presence and I could snag one right out of the water.

I reminded myself that future queens did not catch fish with their bare hands—at least not in Vellana. Here, they sat in gardens looking as pretty as the flowers surrounding them.

"I'm bored," my lady-in-waiting, Lowri, whined, plucking another daisy from the pile and threading it through my silver hair. A ring of tiny white flowers already crowned Lowri's long violet locks, the tips of her pointed ears peeking through.

Me too, I wanted to say.

Instead, I kept my thoughts to myself.

Behind Lowri, Lord Kerrington took a swig from the bottle of wine leftover from our picnic. The basket used for sandwiches and cakes lay empty next to our gilded plates. "Why didn't you say so?" he crooned, wiping his mouth with his shirtsleeve, smearing red across the white material. "I happen to know the cure for boredom."

Lowri's lips quirked into a knowing grin. "Is that so, human?"

My friend collected men the way some women collected shoes—and threw them away with about the same consideration when they were "worn out."

He winked a bloodshot eye, then leaned forward to whisper something that left Lowri's cheeks flushed. If her father knew the way she carried on, he'd have her head. But since he and his wife had chosen not to undergo the three-day voyage from Iodale, he never would.

Lowri tossed the daisies aside and tackled Kerrington to the ground. Their low murmurs and moans were impossible to ignore.

"I'm still here," I reminded them, wiping my wet fingers on one of the lace serviettes beside a half-drunk glass of faerie wine. Although we'd brought twenty crates of the drink with us on the boat last month, the bottles were nearly gone.

"You're more than welcome to join us," Kerrington muttered before kissing Lowri again.

My fiancé's best friend was the worst of rogues, with a mischievous gleam in his mossy green eyes. Lowri had met her match there. Kerrington was meant to follow in his father's footsteps as one of the king's advisors, but it appeared his interests revolved around more carnal pursuits. I'd told Lowri as much, that getting involved with someone like him could only lead to heartache. She'd shrugged, claiming he was a mere distraction until she found her own happily-ever-after.

A young maid with brown hair appeared on the path between two laurel hedges, her arms laden with a tray of tea cakes to replenish the ones we'd already eaten. Although the food in this country lacked flavor, the desserts were palatable enough. Her gray skirt swayed when she stopped to set the tray beside the empty one. Glasses and dishes clinked together as she gathered the remnants from our picnic.

She looked the same as the other maids who flitted around the castle: white apron, white mop cap, gleaming black boots—

Not gleaming. Hole-ridden and coming apart at the seams.

Kerrington shoved Lowri off his lap to grin at the newcomer. "And who do we have here?"

Lowri adjusted the front of her cornflower blue dress, a deep blush creeping up her throat. "You heard him. What's your name, girl?"

"I-it's Falin, milady," the maid stuttered, giving us a terrible curtsy.

"Was that meant to be a curtsy?" Lowri laughed. "And what is the matter with your boots? It's a wonder they let someone so slovenly work in the castle."

I understood Lowri's sudden ire after some of the

vicious slurs and outright disdain I'd been forced to endure since our arrival.

Not a drop of royal blood.

Stealing our throne.

Used magic to wheedle her way into our prince's heart.

I'd even overheard two courtiers saying I had ears like a troll. I could fashion a glamour to hide them, but why? So the humans could be more comfortable around me because I looked like them? Who cared what my ears looked like? They didn't have any bearing on how I would one day rule as queen.

The humans would get used to it eventually, especially once more fae returned to Vellana.

Until then, Lowri, my mother, and I were the only three fae on the island. We needed to stick together and prove that we wouldn't cower in light of anyone's disdain for us. Still, this particular maid had done nothing wrong.

Lowri tapped her feet in delight, her silver slippers sparkling in the sunlight as she plucked a tea cake from the platter, took a bite, then spat it in the grass next to the servant's decrepit boots. "Did you make these?"

"Y-yes, milady."

"Well, they're revolting."

"Lowri . . ." I started to reprimand her, but the words stuck in my throat, caught between loyalty to my best friend —to the fae—and what I knew in my heart was right. Calling her out in front of Kerrington and the maid would do more harm than good. I'd speak with her tonight when we no longer had an audience.

Kerrington took a massive bite of his own cake. "I think they're excellent."

Lowri grabbed another cake and smashed it on his head, collapsing in a fit of giggles at his indignant snort.

Kerrington removed the smashed cake from his head to eat it, washing the morsel down with the bottle of wine, seeming unbothered by the way the frosting clung to his red hair.

A dark figure rounded the hedge, and I resisted the urge to groan. As much as I loved the idea of being queen, there were some downsides. Namely one tall, black-haired, evil downside.

Prince Caiman.

My love's terrible younger brother, and the worst of the fae haters. The awful things he'd said about me had taught me a valuable lesson in trusting the wrong man. One I would not soon forget.

The maid bobbed another pitiful curtsy and ran off toward the castle.

"Oh, lovely," Lowri drawled, flopping onto her stomach to collect her glass of wine, her turquoise eyes landing on me. "Your stalker is back."

Tucking his gloved hands into the pockets of his black trousers, Caiman gave Lowri a vicious sneer. "For the size of your head, Lowri, there's not an original thought in it. You really must come up with some new insults."

Her cheeks burned brighter than Kerrington's hair. "Go jump off a cliff, Prince of Darkness."

No sense intervening in this fight. Caiman deserved every bit of hatred he received—and then some.

Once, I'd foolishly thought him handsome, with his strange onyx eyes and black hair that often escaped its leather queue. Back when I first met both brothers, sixteen-year-old Alrec had been arrogant and loud, constantly bragging about his accomplishments. The polar opposite to his quiet, thoughtful brother Caiman.

I almost laughed. Caiman was quiet, all right. Like a

panther stalking its prey, just waiting to maul his unsuspecting victim and rip out her heart.

When the time came for me to select which prince was to be my husband, Caiman had made the choice simple.

"Is my little brother bothering you again, my love?" a smooth voice drawled.

The dark thoughts in my mind evaporated as Alrec strolled into view, his white shirt unbuttoned at the collar, revealing a corner of the tattoo he'd gotten on his twentieth birthday: a soaring eagle with its wings spread wide. His family's crest.

A vision of power and grace, the future king of Vellana's golden hair reached to his broad shoulders. His red waistcoat with golden buttons hung open.

Behind him, Broderick, his faithful guard, waited in his red and gold uniform, stoic and silent as ever, without so much as a smile or a nod in greeting. His brown hair had been cropped short, a style popular among the other guards and soldiers at the castle.

I glanced toward Caiman to find him watching me through his unnerving eyes. It felt like they could see into my soul . . . and found me lacking. The way he could cut me down with a look made me want to hurl a rock at his smug face.

Lowri pointed at Caiman. "Look at the way he stares at you. He's obsessed."

Smiling, I rose and spread my periwinkle skirts to cover my bare feet. "I know. It's positively vile. Go find someone else to pine over." I took Alrec's hand, the smooth heat of his skin sending chills of sweet anticipation down my spine.

Caiman chuckled darkly. "You think I pine over someone like you?"

She's a monster.

An abomination.

Rage burned like alcohol-soaked kindling in my chest. I tamped it down. Way, *way* down. Losing my composure would only serve as fodder for the awful prince and give him another reason to claim I wasn't fit for Vellana's throne. "I suggest you hold your tongue—unless you wish for your brother to teach you another 'lesson'?"

Every time I visited, I'd heard new accounts of Caiman's wickedness, each one more wretched than the last. If Alrec hadn't been around to keep him in line, there was no telling what atrocities he would've committed.

Caiman's lips curled into a sneer. "Just when I think you couldn't disgust me more." He turned on his heel, all ramrod-straight posture and formality.

Good riddance.

A tea cake flew through the air, splattering white icing down the center of his back.

Kerrington, Lowri, and Alrec burst out laughing. Caiman didn't bother acknowledging any of them as he stalked past Broderick toward the castle.

Lowri glanced from beneath her lashes at the handsome lord brushing crumbs from his dark green breeches. When Kerrington caught her watching, he dragged her on top of him to pick up where they'd left off.

Alrec's grip on my hand tightened, and he pulled me away from the water, past the central fountain, and beneath a line of rose-covered trellises. Pink and white petals sprinkled the path like fallen snow, soft as a carpet beneath my feet. Bees buzzed, flitting from flower to flower. With the thick tangle of thorns and leaves keeping the breeze from reaching us, sweat collected at the back of my neck beneath the heavy curtain of my hair.

"You can stay there, Brod," Alrec threw over his shoulder before the guard could join us.

When Alrec turned back, he drew me close, pressing his lips to mine. The stubble of his short beard scratched my chin, and his tongue tasted of smoky whiskey. "I've missed you," he murmured, his hands slipping to my backside, pulling me hard against him.

"Easy there, your highness," I laughed, relocating his hands to my hips. "We're not married yet."

He shifted his attention to the delicate skin of my earlobe. "This will be the longest four weeks of my life."

The heat pooling in my stomach had nothing to do with it being summertime. "It'll be worth the wait," I reminded him—and myself. Four weeks until forever. Four weeks until I was his and he was mine.

Groaning, he combed a hand through his hair. "I know it will, my love. I know. Please forgive my ardor. It has been a trying day of meetings. The only thing that got me through was knowing I'd see you when it was all over."

Seeing him, spending time with him, falling deeper and deeper in love with his passion and generosity was my favorite part of every day. The arrogant young man from four years ago had grown into a strong, confident leader. Although with all his duties, we rarely had a moment alone to get to know one another properly. The joys of marrying a future king.

After growing up in a small, secluded village in the north of Iodale, I'd been so nervous to meet a human. The fae had been exiled from Vellana, along with magic, by one of the previous kings. Then, five years ago, King Bedwyr became gravely ill. Although his wife at the time sought the best healers in Vellana, no one could cure what ailed him.

The king learned of a clan of powerful fae living only a

three-day voyage south, my mother the greatest healer among them. When his men came with trunks of gold, she had turned them away. Immortal fae had long memories, and she had been a child when the Danú, creatures with magic in their blood, were banished from Vellana, left to flee for their lives to the neighboring islands of Airren and Iodale.

But the king's men were persistent. After a week, she agreed to heal the king in exchange for a promise: that I would be matched with one of his sons as a sign of peace between the humans and fae. As part of the deal, his kingdom had to welcome the fae—and their magic—back to Vellana's shores.

This alliance would be the first step in healing the deep rift between our people, the devastation of which my mother had witnessed first-hand.

I traced the lines of Alrec's tattoo, half expecting the deep blue feathers to feel downy soft. "What sort of meetings?"

The corners of Alrec's sky-blue eyes crinkled when he smiled. "Nothing for you to worry about, my fae bride."

Over the last four years, I had been educated in politics, battle strategy, and foreign relations. In Vellana, however, it seemed women were more ornaments than partners. I'd find a way to change that, to make my future husband under-stand that my being a woman wasn't a weakness but a strength.

"Would it be all right if I joined you next time?" I pressed.

His lips flattened. "Whatever for?"

"To learn more about the country I am to help rule."

"Let us speak of this after we are wed."

I closed my eyes, making a mental note to bring it up the

day after we exchanged vows. I didn't want him believing I was content to sit idly by while he ruled on his own. "There is one more thing I would like to discuss." I resumed tracing his tattoo, loving the way his skin broke into goosebumps, breathing in the woodsy scent clinging to his shirt. "It involves the castle servants."

Alrec's light brows pinched together, his hand landing atop mine, stilling my movements. "Are you having trouble again?"

When we'd first arrived, one maid had spoken out against being assigned to Lowri. I'd brought the matter to Alrec's attention, and he'd swooped in and had the woman removed from the castle entirely.

"No, nothing like that. It's just . . ." How did I say this without him taking offense? "I would like to learn about the staff's wages. How much they earn in each position and such." My mother always said that servants were the lifeblood of any household. Finding and keeping those who were truly loyal was of the upmost importance.

If the young maid we'd met today didn't have the funds to purchase proper work attire, then she may not have the funds to provide for her own welfare. Poverty was a blight on any nation. We should be doing everything in our power to help those who struggled.

"There's no need to concern yourself with such trivial matters, my love. We have a man in charge of such things. Now." Alrec withdrew a shimmering necklace with diamonds the size of my thumbnail from his coat pocket. "I saw this lying among the queen's jewels and it made me think of you." He turned me so my back was to him, brushing my hair aside to fasten the necklace at my throat, the center jewel like an icy weight against my breastbone.

"My beautiful diamond," Alrec whispered, pressing a kiss to my temple.

I pinned a smile on my face, reminding myself how lucky I was. People searched their whole lives for something I'd found at only eighteen.

And in four more weeks, I would have my happily-ever-after.

2

CAIMAN

I'VE HEARD IT SAID THAT A WOMAN COULD BE LIKE THE SUN, giving light and warmth to those around her. My brother's betrothed was like the sun because she burned those who fell out of her favor. The beautiful fae lit hearts ablaze and danced around the writhing flames until they were nothing more than ash and embers.

And mine happened to be her favorite kindling.

There was a time when she'd looked upon me with smiles that touched her stunning silver eyes. Then everything changed.

She'd been given a choice between the golden god who could give her a throne or me, a useless second son with nothing to offer but my heart. I'd been convinced Roisin was different from other women, that she'd been able to see through my brother's glorious façade to the monster lurking beneath.

Turned out she'd fallen under his spell as easily as everyone else.

Loud music rattled through my brain. Too many bodies surged toward the dance floor, making the already humid air unbearable. If I could have skipped the whole vapid ball, I would have. Unfortunately, it was my duty as the spare heir to sit here like an ornament and watch everyone else enjoy themselves.

Everyone except my brother's personal guard, Broderick.

The poor man was misery incarnate where he stood, steely gaze fixed on Alrec as he danced with any and every maiden he could find. As the future king, it was customary to entertain the females of the kingdom with a dance, but he'd neglected his fiancée ever since she'd arrived with her vacuous lady-in-waiting in tow.

I had no fondness for women like Lowri—the ones more interested in wealth and stature than morals or character. Then again, considering who her mistress was, such an attitude should've come as no surprise.

When Lord Kerrington saw the purple-haired fae, he dropped his glass of champagne on an empty table and snapped her up for a dance. I couldn't stand the spoiled bastard. If it were up to me, he'd be stripped of his title and sent to the army's front lines without a weapon. I'd pay good money to see how his silver tongue fared in war.

The three of them forgot themselves far too often. Forgot that my father was king and could punish them for speaking to me as disrespectfully as they did. But they were untouchable because of their connection to my brother. The future king of Vellana.

What must it be like, to wake up and have nothing better to do than lounge all day in beautiful gowns, feast on cakes, and attend parties? To want nothing more for yourself? If only I could be content doing the same. Instead, I kept myself busy making plans for how to escape and serve my country from afar.

"You really should smile more," my father, King Bedwyr, muttered from his throne. It could've been a trick of the candlelight, but his golden hair and beard seemed threaded with more white than the day before, and the wrinkles across his brow appeared more pronounced. "Ladies love a man who smiles." His own lips lifted into a dazzling smile that had won him the hearts of not one but four wives. The first had passed away in childbirth, the second in a tragic carriage accident. The third, Alrec's mother, fell victim to a terrible disease. And the last, my own mother, had succumbed to wasting sickness only a day before Lady Roisin's mother had arrived to heal her.

I shifted on my small wooden throne—if one could call it that. It was little more than a fancy dining chair. "I smile."

"No, you scowl."

I did that as well, but only because I didn't have it in me to play false. I smiled when I was happy. Which wasn't often since enemy ships had been spotted off the southern coast, near Southbay. The lords there grew restless, begging for reinforcements in case the continental king decided to attack. Because of my brother, we'd spent the better part of today locked in the council chambers discussing how many of our men to send. Alrec thought of war as moving pawns in a game of chess. But our soldiers weren't pawns. They were men with lives and families and people who loved them. Every time he brought up war, I'd attempted to bring the conversation back to maintaining peace.

"See. You're doing it right now." My father gestured to my face with a bejeweled hand. "You really should be more like your brother."

Alrec was the last person on this island I wanted to

emulate. Still, I forced a smile for my father's benefit as I searched the dance floor for the kingdom's heir.

Alrec had finally claimed his bride-to-be. The way he held her left my chest aching. Every night, I swore I wouldn't let seeing the two of them together get to me. I would encase my heart in steel where no one could touch it. But even steel melts when it finds enough heat.

And Roisin made me burn.

Roisin's mother watched from beside one of the leaded windows, her eternally youthful face content. The handful of times we'd spoken, Lady Seren had been kind. The exact opposite of her daughter.

My father waved for one of the footmen to refill his gold goblet with faerie wine. From the glassy-eyed look he offered, it was clear he'd already consumed far too much. Still, it wasn't my place to admonish the king.

"Go, dance and have fun," he commanded. The rings on his fingers glinted when he gestured toward the dance floor. "Your responsibilities will still be there tomorrow."

I shoved to my feet and started for one of the servants carrying trays of bubbling champagne, planning to have a drink and wander amongst the tittering courtiers for a bit before slipping away to my chambers. It wasn't as if anyone would notice my absence.

The servant stopped when he saw me approach, a single glass remaining on his tray. I reached for it, but a slender hand grabbed the flute before I could. A hand belonging to the one woman I'd been hoping to avoid.

Roisin's eyes widened at first, then her surprise was quickly hidden beneath a sneer. "Well, if it isn't the Prince of Darkness." The pink stain on her lips left a mark on the glass's delicate edge when she took a sip. The frothy blue dress she wore reminded me of a wispy cloud.

Her beauty stole my breath every single time. It wasn't just her silvery hair that set her apart from other women I'd met. A faint glow of magic emanated from her warm, tanned skin. The light of life twinkled in her quicksilver eyes. "Always a pleasure seeing you, Lady Roisin."

"Feigning niceties now, are we?" she returned.

"Probably for the best considering the size of our audience." I tucked my hands into my pockets to hide their trembling. Each time we met was like tearing open an old scar. The wound used to have time to heal between visits, but now that she lived here, the pain in my chest had become a constant reminder that I hadn't been enough for her.

I should've been used to it by now. But coming second best in everything else was nothing compared to being passed up by this woman, watching her slip her hand into Alrec's, claiming him as her future husband.

He's the heir.

You couldn't possibly think I would choose you over him.

"I'd rather converse with a smelly fish monger," she muttered under her breath.

"And I'd rather converse with a rotting corpse."

The flute of golden liquid shook in her clenched fist. "I know exactly what you're doing, but you will not win."

What in heaven's name was she talking about?

"You are trying to unnerve me. Force me to lose my composure in front of all these people to prove I would make a terrible queen."

Where had she come up with that load of nonsense? As much as it pained me to admit it, Roisin was just what Vellana needed to bring us closer to our allies in Iodale and align ourselves with the powerful fae across our territories.

My only concern was that she had to marry the devil himself to take the throne.

She huffed a breath, fluttering the curls framing her heart-shaped face. "I know you and I—" Her words stopped abruptly when two courtiers passed us with raised brows. "I know you and I have history," she continued in a harsh whisper once we were alone again. As alone as two people could be in a crowd, anyway. "But I think it would be best if we put our past behind us and move forward without all of this animosity."

"What history would that be?" The time she'd claimed I'd tripped her and Alrec had given me a black eye? Or the day she threw her drink in my face? Maybe she was referring to the time I'd accidentally bumped into Lowri, and Alrec had burned my mother's first-edition Hawthorne to teach me one of his "lessons."

"The day you kissed me."

The dancing, the chatter, the clinking of glasses all fell silent beneath the roaring in my ears. As if he'd heard her, Alrec turned from where he was speaking with Kerrington, his eyes darting between me and his bride-to-be. "You must be mistaking me for someone else," I said. "I have never—and would never—dream of kissing someone like you."

"Someone like me?" she hissed, her skin brightening with the heat of anger. "You human *pig*. When I am queen, I will have you locked in the dungeons and left to rot."

By the time she took the throne, I would be long gone.

"Ah, Caiman." A heavy hand slammed over my shoulder. Alrec's narrowed eyes found mine. "I thought I told you to leave my things alone."

His things. That's what he called his fiancée. And Roisin stood there, glaring as if I were the villain. Broderick stalked toward us, eyes fastened on me and a hand on the pommel of his sword. Like I'd try anything in a crowd full of people.

I smiled, hoping my father could see it from his throne. "Your *thing* approached me."

Alrec gave Roisin a pointed scowl. "Is that true, my love?"

"For all I know, he saw me heading this way and ambushed me. You know he's been obsessed with me for years."

Why did everyone keep saying that? I was *not* obsessed with her. "I'm the one obsessed with you, am I? You're the one claiming we ki—"

Roisin's hand shot out, catching my wrist. "I should probably dance with him to put him out of his misery." She tugged me toward the dance floor.

The quadrille that had been playing ended on a high, and the spinning couples glistening with sweat began to clap. "What's wrong, Roisin? Does your 'beloved' not know you've been fantasizing about kissing me?"

The quartet began a waltz—my least favorite dance of the lot.

Her grip on my wrist cut off the bloodflow to my fingers. "You are a pig."

We stopped in the center of the floor beneath the mammoth chandelier. Damn it all if she didn't smell divine, like candied roses. "You said that already."

"Let's just get this over with so I can go back to Alrec." She settled one hand on my shoulder and offered me the other.

The heat of her fingers burned straight through the layers to my skin beneath. Lowri and Kerrington watched us from beside Alrec. My brother's massive arms folded over his chest, his eyes narrowing into slits. This wasn't worth whatever punishment he thought I'd deserve for touching his *things*.

I drew away, ignoring the shocked glares and gasps from the lords and ladies waltzing around us. "I'd rather be hung, drawn, and quartered."

Roisin's mouth dropped open. I could feel her blazing eyes boring into my back as I turned and started for the dais where my father sat, smiling out at his subjects as they celebrated the heir's upcoming nuptials. I climbed the three steps to take my place on his left.

"There now, my boy." My father's voice crackled when his weathered hand patted my forearm. "Wasn't that pleasant?"

It was certainly something.

"Don't you worry. Once your brother is wed, we will find you a wife."

For some reason, my eyes found Roisin where she danced with Alrec. He'd probably swooped in like the hero she thought he was, saving her from the embarrassment I'd caused.

"And if I do not wish to marry?" Women had been paraded in front of me like prized cattle my entire life, and I hadn't been interested in any of them except one.

My father's hand shook as he lifted his golden goblet to his lips. "You are young. You will change your mind."

Again, I found Roisin, giggling with Lowri as Kerrington and my brother waltzed together, much to the amusement of those around them. Her chiming laughter cut through everything, striking my ears like church bells at Yule.

"I don't think I will." No, my life was destined to be lived alone. But if I played my cards right, I could be living alone far from this castle.

With all the unrest in the south, my father planned to

send an emissary to the continent to try and smooth things over with King Tarren. A position I was more than qualified —and more than happy—to fill.

If I could only get up the nerve to ask.

Something crashed beside me. My father's goblet fell onto the small table, spilling greenish-yellow liquid all over the marble surface. The king's hand flew to his chest, clutching at the gold chain holding his mantle in place.

"Father?" I shot to my feet, watching in horror as he gasped for breath. "Father!" I caught him when he slumped forward. The guards surrounding the dais sprang into action, closing us off from view. The music came to a screeching halt, replaced by harsh whispers and feminine wails.

What could be wrong? The goblet. Had someone poisoned him?

Alrec's cursing exploded through the pounding in my ears. He knocked the guards aside and dropped to his knees, reaching for our father's limp hand. "What is it? What's happened?"

I clutched our father closer, clinging to his heavy doublet as if he could save me from the pain lancing through my chest. "I don't know. He was fine one moment, then he collapsed."

Alrec shoved me out of the way, taking our father's body onto his own lap, removing the clasp on the chain, and letting the thick mantle fall to the dais. "What did you say to him? What did you do? You must've done something."

"I didn't do a blasted thing!" Tears clouded my vision, and I swore I saw a woman with black hair lying next to me, staring at the muraled ceiling through sightless brown eyes. I scrubbed at my face, helplessness washing over me when my father's prone form came back into focus.

Roisin stood beside Lady Lowri at the foot of the dais, a trembling hand pressed against her lips.

This wasn't like the last time.

Last time, help had arrived too late.

"Get your mother," I shouted to Roisin. "Now!"

She turned and ran through the crowd. I had known this day would come but had hoped it would be decades down the line.

It wouldn't be long before my brother became the King of Vellana.

3

ROISIN

THE GOLDEN CLOCK IN THE CORNER BENEATH THE KING'S crest ticked away the seconds like a metronome. I flexed my toes inside too-tight slippers, wishing I was barefoot on the plush rug stretching across the floor in the king's bedchamber.

It felt surreal seeing such a strong, powerful man age decades in a matter of hours. When we'd arrived at the ball, he'd been in high spirits, greeting myself and my mother with an exuberant hug. Now he lay prone in a massive four-poster bed, his face the same pale shade as the sheets beneath him.

Alrec waited at his father's bedside, his handsome features schooled into a thoughtful mask as he watched the royal physician examine the king. The stooped old man ignored my mother and I while we waited by the window, bringing item after item out of a black leather bag. The most heinous of them was a cylindrical tube with sharp spikes protruding from the bottom. I wasn't sure what that was for, but I hoped I wouldn't have to see the man use it.

Eventually he found a wooden horn fluted on both ends.

He pressed one end to the King's chest and the other to his ear. I held my breath, afraid to make a noise. When he told the king to inhale, the king's ragged gasp left my knees trembling.

I glanced at my mother, checking to see if she appeared well. There were perhaps a few more wrinkles around her eyes—silver like my own. And the smile lines around her mouth had deepened. Other than that, she appeared the same as she always had. What if I was wrong, though? What if she collapsed out of the blue? It was one thing for her to return to Iodale and another thing entirely to imagine going on without her forever.

The physician moved on to another tool from his bag. This one he used to check the king's tongue and throat. This sort of medicine was foreign to me. Fae rarely got sick unless they encountered some sort of poison. And by the time one noticed the symptoms, it was usually too late. We could be killed by other means, of course, but if the wounds weren't fatal, our innate magic healed us before any real damage could be done. There were true immortals among us, ones powerful enough to return from death. But they were few and far between.

Caiman sat on a chair in the corner, elbows resting on his knees as he stared toward the dark shadows above the bed.

"I have never—and would never—dream of kissing someone like you."

Someone like me. A fae.

The snide comment shouldn't have stung. I'd heard far worse shouted by the crowds in the city. For some reason, the insults always struck deeper coming from him. I didn't know why. I should've been used to it by now.

The first time I'd come to Vellana, my mother and I had

met Alrec and his father for a hunting excursion, and we'd spent a week "getting to know one another." Meaning Alrec would kill some poor animal and boast about it until the following day when he would kill another. Although he'd been handsome, he'd also been arrogant and, if I was being honest, a little irritating. After our visit, my mother and I traveled to the castle to meet the younger prince and the queen.

Considering Alrec's personality, I'd had very low expectations. My mother had only smiled as she always did, serenely and with a hit of knowing, and told me to give him a chance. Caiman had been so quiet, sitting on the stairs with a book in his hands. A dark-haired teen with strange eyes who ended up surprising me at every turn. If only I'd known then that those black eyes reflected his black heart.

"It appears as though this is a fleeting ailment, your highness," the physician said in a gravelly voice, propping his veiny hands on top of his leather bag. "After a week abed, you should be fit to rule again."

"Thank you, Mortimer," said the king, his typically booming voice meek and mild. "As always, your faithful service to the crown is most appreciated. However, I do feel I would benefit from a second opinion." The king's head turned toward the window. "Lady Seren?"

The physician visibly bristled, but he bowed his head before shoving his instruments back into his bag. When he finished, instead of leaving, he stalked to the corner to wait beside Caiman.

My mother removed her elbow-length gloves, tucking them into the small purse dangling from her wrist. "If your highness wouldn't mind, I would like my daughter's help."

"She is to be my daughter as well." The king waved me forward. "Let her come to me."

I followed my mother to the king's bedside, awaiting instruction. My mother had seen battles, healed warriors on the brink of death. Having never witnessed the horrors of war, I wasn't as adept at healing, but she had taught me the basics. If I hadn't been matched with the prince, I would've followed in her footsteps as a healer. Now, I would serve the world in a different way.

My mother took the king's large hand in her own and closed her eyes. Her skin began to glow as her healing magic passed through her body to his. If she gave too much, she'd be the one in bed for the week.

Her eyes snapped open, and her brow furrowed. "Roisin, take his hand." She gave over the king's hand and sank onto the mattress, sliding her hands beneath the neck of his white tunic, covering his heart.

I closed my own eyes and let the heat of magic inside me swell like a river in a rainstorm, channeling the warmth through my veins toward the king. Heat reached my fingertips . . . and stopped. I tried to force it beyond whatever invisible barrier kept us apart, but it refused to pass. When I opened my eyes again, I met my mother's panicked gaze.

Folding his arms over his chest, Alrec shifted his weight from one foot to the other. The golden waistcoat he'd discarded at the foot of the bed glittered in the lamplight. "Well? What is it? What's wrong with him?"

My mother smoothed her hands down her skirts. No one else seemed to notice the way they trembled. "I'm afraid the news is grave."

I'd forgotten I was holding the king's hand until his fingers contracted, wrapping around mine.

My mother's lips pursed, as if she were trying to find the right words. "Your highness, it's your heart. It's failing."

Alrec stepped forward, his boot colliding with the

bedframe. "You must be wrong. Sir Mortimer said he would be fine in a week."

The physician sneered from his place next to the wall. All Caiman did was stare at his father.

"With all due respect to Sir Mortimer," my mother said carefully, bowing her head as if she were beneath him when she had a hundred years more experience than the insufferable doctor, "he does not have my skills."

"Skills?" Alrec dashed a hand through his hair. "If you had any skills to speak of, you would heal him."

"If he was suffering from a disease, I could. But this is a fight he cannot win, one against time and age. Man was not created to last forever, and his heart is tired."

"That's a load of bollocks."

"Alrec!" The king withdrew his hand from my grasp, his eyes narrowed on his son. "You dare speak to your future mother-in-law that way? This woman has healed me more times than I can count. If she says my heart is failing, then it must be true."

Alrec's face contorted, and his hands fisted at his sides before he turned on his heel and stalked out of the chamber, the physician following close behind. Caiman remained so still, so silent, I had forgotten he was there. As if he knew I was thinking about him, his dark eyes lifted to mine.

My stomach fluttered, and it took all my strength to turn away. He had no right to look at me like that. Like he wasn't an awful pig. Like he was someone worth caring about.

"There's no sense staring at a dying man," the king said with a weak smile. "Get back to the party and assure everyone that I am well."

What must it be like, knowing one was nearing the end of his life? Fae could live for hundreds, even thousands of years. Part of my betrothal contract stipulated that once

Alrec had passed, my reign as queen would end and our son would take the throne. Assuming we had a son. I shook away the errant thought. There would be plenty of time to worry about that later. Right now, I needed to find my fiancé and make sure he was all right.

My mother and I started for the privy chamber adjoining the bedroom. Caiman finally moved, taking my mother's place on the bed beside the king.

The door fell closed with a quiet click.

"Did you feel it?" she whispered as we passed the ornate furniture scattered around the candlelit chamber, decorated in the same deep golds and reds as the rest of the King's private quarters.

I skirted around a tête-à-tête , narrowly avoiding ramming into its scrolled arms. "I did. It felt as though my magic was blocked." With the handful of people I'd healed before, my magic had passed seamlessly between us. Then again, those wounds had been superficial, a broken bone here, a cut or gash there. The worst had been the time Lowri had gouged her leg on a rusted nail protruding from an old fence. Her parents were fae, but her ancestors had intermixed with humans, weakening their magic through the years, so she hadn't been strong enough to quickly heal on her own. Terrified of having a nasty scar, she'd begged me to help. As if she'd needed to beg. She was my dearest friend. I would've done it regardless.

"I've felt it when men on the battlefield were too far gone to save," she explained. "When that happens, all we can do is make them comfortable."

"Isn't there any way to save him?" It wasn't that I doubted my mother, but the king seemed like a good man, and his people loved him. We needed to exhaust all avenues before giving up.

Her silver eyes flashed to the door before returning to me. "There is one thing." Her voice dropped to a whisper. "If you managed to force your magic past the block, it would heal him. But our legends say that it would drain you of your immortality."

In the silence, I could hear my own heart pounding in my ears. Alrec had been right. There was a way to save the king, but it would cost my mother her immortal life. As much as I had come to care for King Bedwyr as a leader and even a father figure, I wouldn't trade my mother's life for his. Perhaps it was selfish because he was a king, needed by his people, but I needed my mother more.

My mother gripped my shoulders, giving me a gentle shake. "You cannot tell the humans, Roisin. Do you understand?"

"I won't tell, Mum. I swear—"

The door to the king's chambers creaked open. Caiman came out, seeming startled to find us still in the room. "Lady Seren, may I have a word?" His black eyes flicked to me. "Alone."

Gritting my teeth, I stomped to the door. I didn't stop until I'd made it through the king's study and into the cavernous hallway.

The sconces on the wall flickered, highlighting Alrec and Lord Kerrington deep in discussion next to a bust of a previous monarch. Broderick stood against the opposite wall, staring blankly ahead like the statue.

Alrec rushed to my side, collecting me in the warmth of his strong embrace.

"I'm so sorry about your father," I told him. "So very, very sorry."

"There's no need to be sorry, my love. As your mother

said, there is nothing to be done. My father is an old man. He's survived four wives and lived a full and happy life."

The end of a life, even a long and happy one, was still a tragedy. The twisting weight of guilt churned with my sorrow. My mother didn't have to be the one to sacrifice herself. It could've been me.

"Come, you two lovebirds." Lord Kerrington slapped my fiancé's back. "Your father would want us to return to the party."

Alrec laced our fingers together. I was about to go with him when my mother emerged from the King's study.

"I will join you in a moment," I told them, letting Alrec's hand fall. He gave me a smile that set my heart alight before leaving with Kerrington and his silent guard. I hurried to my mother's side, my worry compounding when I found her eyes filled with tears.

"What's wrong? If Caiman was rude to you, I swear—" I'd do worse than throw him in the dungeon. I'd have the pig roasted on a spit.

"Rude?" My mother dabbed at the corners of her eyes with a handkerchief that had a tiny black "C" embroidered in the corner. "My dear girl, Prince Caiman was the only one who thanked me."

4

CAIMAN

As a little boy, I looked upon my father with awe. He was a giant among men. There was no battle he couldn't win, no problem too difficult for him to solve. King Bedwyr appeared truly invincible. After last night's sobering news, I had to come to terms with another harsh reality of this cruel world.

Even the most invincible man is still only a man—a bag of skin and bones encasing a failing heart.

My father was dying.

In hindsight, the revelation shouldn't have come as a shock. Although he looked closer to sixty, the man must've been pushing ninety. I knew he'd been healed before by Lady Seren, but after speaking with her in the privy chamber, I realized my father had called for her services on numerous occasions, ridding himself of all manner of sicknesses. Chest infections, gout, cholera, whooping cough, influenza, and even an abscess tooth.

The one thing even King Bedwyr couldn't outrun: time.

I squinted against the bright sunshine as I made my way to the stables, seeking an escape from the darkness that had fallen over the castle. Tugging my gloves tighter onto my fingers, I rounded the corner to find my brother seated on his white stallion. His white-on-white attire coupled with a ridiculous gold coat made him look like a bloomin' archangel.

And wouldn't you know, his fiancée had dressed to match, all white lace and gold accents, like a bride on her wedding day. The perfect pair on matching steeds.

Lowri's green frock contrasted with Kerrington's waistcoat the color of aubergines. Broderick and four other guards in red and gold livery rounded out the riding party. Although Vellana was relatively safe, we typically traveled with twice that many soldiers in case we met trouble. Perhaps they were going on a short jaunt around the castle.

I didn't bother asking because I didn't care.

One of the stable boys milling about the yard rushed to collect my horse from where she'd been tethered to a post, lapping at the trough.

Alrec's icy blue gaze landed on me, and the smile that brightened his bearded face told me everything I needed to know about how this conversation was about to go.

"Ah, brother. So good of you to join us for our ride into the city."

If he was going to the city, they needed more soldiers. Two per person at least. *None of my business*, I reminded myself. "I was actually on my way to the seaside."

"Nonsense. You will accompany us." He lifted his brows, a silent challenge.

I had been putting off asking my father to appoint me as emissary to the continent for months, telling myself I would do it after the hullabaloo with Alrec's wedding had passed. Now, with Father so unwell, I couldn't leave him. And when he passed, I'd need Alrec's permission.

If I wanted any chance of him granting my request, I had no choice but to appease him. A hellish ride into the bowels of the stifling city with miserable company was a small price to pay for freedom.

My mare gave a knicker of acknowledgement as I approached, her musky scent mixed with that of the leather from the saddle calming in its familiarity. Alrec didn't wait for me to mount, kicking his horse immediately toward the red portcullis wedged between the castle's high walls. Our party traveled two by two, a pair of guards at the front, Alrec and Roisin behind them. Lowri and Kerrington exchanged flirtatious banter as their horses fell in step. I urged my mount next to Broderick—the most tolerable of the lot—while the final two guards took up the post at our backs.

We traversed the path winding down toward a picturesque city nestled among burnished hills. Unfortunately, Broderick's stoic silence made it easier to overhear my brother's boasting about his "grand plans" for the kingdom.

First, he planned on winning the war in the south. A war that had yet to begin. A war that could still be avoided—that *should* be avoided at all costs. Next, he wanted to commission a statue commemorating the victory. Finally, he wished to conquer more territory for Vellana, as if the three islands we controlled weren't enough to handle. Did he honestly believe we had troops to spare for such endeavors? Our army was strong, as was our naval fleet, but we needed them here, protecting our people, not off gallivanting trying to collect more.

Thankfully, Alrec managed to reign himself in when we reached the old gates marking the outskirts of the ancient walled city. Red clay rooftops sloped toward white-walled buildings, nearly every one adorned with window boxes overflowing with colorful blooms. Cobbled streets corkscrewed toward the square, where the space came alive with music and chatter. Although we were a few miles north of the port, an occasional breeze carried the perfume of a salty sea, reminding me of my abandoned plans as sweat painted my back.

We dismounted at the edge of a pedestrian street, Alrec catching Roisin by the waist to help her down from her saddle. Lowri looked to Kerrington as if she expected the wastrel to do the same, giving a huff of irritation when she found him too busy picking lint from his breeches. I bit back my smile. Maybe today would be entertaining after all.

One of the guards stayed behind with the horses, while the other three accompanied us into the fray of now-gawking onlookers bobbing curtsies, bowing low, and singing choruses of, "God save the King."

I knew they meant my father, but Alrec smiled and waved as if they were speaking to him. From his pocket, he withdrew a small pink purse—likely filled with gold coins—and handed it to his bride with a flourish.

Roisin and Lowri popped in and out of shops, giggling over bolts of fabric and lingering over strands of diamonds and pearls. None were as beautiful as the necklace Roisin wore. A necklace I recognized as one my father had given my mother on their fifth wedding anniversary. One that should have been mine to give to my wife.

Seeing as I had no plans to marry, the fact that Alrec had been the one to present it to Roisin shouldn't have bothered me as much as it did.

"How many dresses does a woman need?" I grumbled when we stopped at what must've been the tenth shop.

The corner of Broderick's lips twitched in the closest thing the man had to a smile.

The buzz of excitement grew as more people arrived, word of our visit spreading like the plague. If Alrec had wanted to make a spectacle, he'd succeeded.

"He should've brought more guards."

"I know," Broderick said in a surprisingly deep voice.

I blinked up at him, not believing my own ears. "You can talk."

His dark eyebrows arched toward his short hair.

"I mean, of course you can talk. It's just, I don't believe I've ever heard you say anything." He'd been assigned to my brother for almost four years and not once had I heard him so much as sigh.

It came as no surprise that Broderick didn't respond.

Alrec threw gold around like it was his personal duty to empty our coffers while Lowri clung to Kerrington's arm, whispering and laughing, not seeming to notice the way his gaze snagged on every other passing female.

An hour into our *exhilarating* excursion, a manservant I recognized from the castle came running down the street, straight for the guards at our back. Although he was stopped briefly for questioning, the guards let him pass. Alrec dropped his hand from where it had been resting on Roisin's lower back to take a folded piece of paper from the bowing servant.

He scanned the missive, a smile lifting his lips. I waited for him to explain, to hand over the note. Instead, he stuffed it into his pocket and announced that he and Kerrington had been called back to the castle on urgent business. Then he looked directly at me and said, "You will stay with the womenfolk and ensure they return safely."

Think of your goal. Play along. My leather gloves creaked

when my hands flexed. "Of course." I'd love nothing more than to stand here all bloomin' day with the sun beating down on my head and watch two women buy dresses.

With a smirk, Alrec ordered Broderick to stay as well—much to the man's obvious reluctance—and himself, Kerrington, and the remaining guards marched off toward the horses, leaving me with one lone guard and two glaring fae.

"Come, Lowri, let us find more pleasant company." Roisin threaded her arm through her friend's, and they marched off to the next shop.

By the time we left the shop, the path was thronged with peasants and gentry baking in the afternoon sun, leaving the air ripe with the stench of sweat, unwashed bodies, and cloying floral perfume. Despite the foul air, my stomach howled with hunger when I spotted loaves of freshly baked bread and pastries displayed in a bakery's window across the street. A bakery these people shoving against one another seemed determined to keep us from ever reaching.

"Is that one of the princes?" a woman to my right said in what was likely meant to be a whisper. "It is! What was his name again?"

I'd bet no one forgot Alrec's name.

"Where is Prince Alrec?" another woman asked as if she'd heard my silent musings.

"I see the future queen! I see her!"

Even with his sword drawn, Broderick could do nothing to keep the fray from surging toward us.

Roisin and Lowri smiled and waved at everyone, seeming not a bit bothered by the potential for danger here.

If anyone decided to attack, we'd be defenseless, completely at their mercy. Yes, Broderick could fight, but all I had was a decorative dagger I was useless with, and I was certain Roisin didn't have any weapons strapped beneath the white gown that clung to her curves like—

I swallowed past a sudden lump in my throat. What had Alrec been thinking, leaving the castle with so few guards? *Dammit.* Why hadn't I spoken up?

"She's beautiful," said one woman.

"Stunning creature," said another.

"Enchanting," agreed a young man around my own age with only one leg.

"A vision," his female companion agreed.

A short bull of a man shoved his way through a group of children at the front. My hand fell to my dagger. Before I could draw, he spat at Roisin's feet. "Yer naught more than a pair of fae whores," he snarled, gripping the leather belt around his thick waist. "Get back to yer island where ye belong."

Lowri whirled, turquoise eyes narrowed into slits. "What did you call us?"

Roisin caught her friend's arm, tugging her back toward the shop.

"I'd rather be a fae whore than human filth," Lowri spat.

"Broderick, arrest that man," I shouted over the now-roaring crowd.

The guard moved impossibly fast, catching the black-guard by the collar and slamming him onto the ground. He deserved to rot in the dungeon for the rest of his days.

I gave the bakery one final longing glance before looping my arms around my charges' backs and bringing them back into the dress shop. The handful of customers milling around inside stopped to stare. A woman with a measuring tape draped around her neck stood from her stool next to a lady on a raised platform.

"Is there a back exit?" I asked. Between dress forms, bolts of cloth, half-made dresses and people, it was almost impossible to tell.

"There is, sir. Just there." The woman gestured to a black curtain behind her.

I thanked the woman, but before I could tow my charges toward the curtain, Roisin stepped out of reach. "I am perfectly capable of walking on my own."

Lowri drew closer to me, clutching my arm, tears swimming in her eyes. Crying women made me feel so bloomin' helpless. What were you supposed to do with them? I gave her shoulder an awkward pat. "Don't worry. I'll bring you back home."

For some reason, my attempt at reassurance only made her sob harder.

"This place isn't my home."

"Do not allow one human to turn you against us all." It was that sort of nonsense that had started our war with the fae all those centuries ago.

We made it out the back door, down three uneven wooden stairs, and through an alley to where the horses waited without incident. To my relief, the final guard was still close by. Roisin paused in the street, glancing over her shoulder toward a crowd of people who hadn't noticed us.

I helped a sniffling Lowri onto her horse, not bothering to offer assistance to Roisin since she could do it "on her own." I caught the horn on my mare's saddle, but before I could slip my boot into the stirrup, I saw that Roisin had abandoned her horse and started back down the street, muttering that she would be right back.

That infernal woman. "You cannot go off on your —*dammit.*" I told the young guard to take Lady Lowri back to the castle. I would have to talk some sense into my brother's bloomin' fiancée.

After what had just happened, didn't she realize this city wasn't safe? What could she possibly need to do? The moment I rounded the corner of the building, I found Roisin speaking to a young girl in a tatty brown dress. The girl's eyes glittered with tears as she clutched a pink purse to her chest.

A moment later, Roisin sauntered past, chin lifted and a smile playing on her lips as she approached our horses.

I fell in step beside her, careful to avoid puddles of what smelled like piss. "What was that all about?"

"What was what all about?"

"You gave that girl your purse."

"What girl?"

"The one in the brown dress."

Roisin gave an exaggerated glance over her shoulder. "I see no girl in a brown dress."

And with that, she mounted without assistance and rode off toward the castle, making me wonder if I'd imagined the entire thing.

5

ROISIN

THE SKIN BENEATH ALREC'S BLUE EYES LOOKED BRUISED, THE creases across his brow deepening with his frown. I shifted closer on the settee, reaching for his free hand. "How are you?" I asked, even though the answer was obvious.

He set his teacup on the low table in front of us, forcing a smile. "As well as can be expected. And you?"

After our trip to the city the day before, I'd spent most of the evening consoling a distraught Lowri. When I'd asked Alrec at dinner what was to become of the man who had accosted us, he'd told me that he would handle it.

Whether I was fae or human, there would always be people who hated me. I could only do my best and hope that would be enough to assure the humans that I had Vellana's best interests at heart. "I had some trouble sleeping, but other than that, I am well."

Chuckling, he swiped a hand across his brow. "It's no wonder, with how unseasonably mild it is so close to September. We could take a ride to the seaside if you'd like. There's always a fair breeze along the coast."

The thought of leaving the castle so soon after what had

41

happened left my stomach in knots. I hadn't been scared, per se, but the situation could've gone downhill very fast. Lowri hadn't wanted to set foot out of her room this morning.

A fat bumblebee meandered through the open window, finding one of the many bouquets of fresh blooms decorating the solar.

Alrec squeezed my fingers. "Fear not. I will bring so many guards that you will see red uniforms everywhere you turn."

"Tomorrow, perhaps?"

Sighing, he collected one of the tartlets from a stand beside the gold tea service. Although my own tea had gone cold, I sipped it anyway to rid myself of the dryness in my throat.

"I've meetings tomorrow, I'm afraid."

"What sort of meetings?" I asked, as if I hadn't already heard Alrec speaking of the brewing conflict in the south.

"The sort that vex me," Alrec said around a bite before wiping his hands on a lace serviette. Crumbs dusted the dark blue breeches stretched across his muscular thighs.

Lovely. Another day of sitting around with nothing to do. Who would've thought living in a castle would be so boring?

As much as I'd enjoyed getting out yesterday before everything went pear shaped, all of the dresses ended up looking the same after the third shop. It wasn't as if I needed more garments. I'd simply used shopping as an excuse to spend some time with my fiancé outside of these walls, to try to grow closer in hopes that he might open up to me. That he might see that I could be his partner as well as his love. Then he'd invited Kerrington and suggested I bring Lowri, and all my plans had evaporated.

"Did you receive my gift?" he asked, his hand falling to my knee.

Ah, yes. His gift. This time it was a new pair of gold slippers, delivered to my bedroom before breakfast.

I showed him my feet encased in gold. "I did. And they're beautiful. Thank you." As were all the other gifts he'd given me over the last four years.

His eyes gleamed when he smiled. For some reason, my heart didn't flutter the way it usually did. Must have been the heat.

"Have I told you about the statue I'm having commissioned?"

Heavens above. Not more statue talk. As much as I loved him, his obsession with statues was becoming ridiculous. Still, I pinned a smile to my lips. "Which one?"

Alrec spoke of statues for what felt like forever while servants removed the desserts and tea service, replacing them with a jug of cold water with slices of cucumber floating around in it. The changes I hoped to bring about were more subtle. After running into the maid, Falin, in the city, I was more determined than ever to ensure our castle staff saw a wage increase. I was also considering starting some sort of charity for women in the city who were struggling.

I poured myself a glass of water, drinking until my stomach sloshed, nodding when necessary and offering a few words of agreement, until finally, *finally* Alrec grinned and said he had a surprise for me.

He caught my hand and brought me out into the cool marble hallway, past where Broderick stood, and up into the throne room. The thick red velvet drapes did little to keep our footsteps from echoing against the double-height coffered ceiling. Everything, from the chairs along the wall to the picture frames to the stairs at the foot of the dais, had been painted red or gilded with gold leaf.

On top of the dais sat two ornate gold thrones. One was twice the size of the other, with an eagle's head carved across the back. I'd seen the king sitting there on multiple occasions, welcoming visitors, holding court, hearing the concerns of the people.

I ran my fingertips along the gilded roses carved into the smaller throne's scrolled arms. "Where's the surprise?"

"It's right here." He patted the red velvet cushion on the small throne's seat. "This is to be your throne."

It was beautiful, to be sure. But why was it so bloody small? "The craftmanship is stunning," I said, trying to remain positive.

Alrec rocked back on his heels, tucking his thumbs into his belt loops and puffing out his chest as he surveyed the empty room.

Not empty.

Broderick stood with his back to us at the entrance. When had he arrived?

"I knew you'd love it," Alrec announced. "Commissioned it myself the year before last. It only just arrived. And right in the nick of time too, with my father's failing health."

My mother had been to see the king last night. When I'd asked after him, she'd shaken her head and said he didn't have long. "How is the king today?"

Alrec's shoulders lifted with his sigh. "Much the same, I'm afraid. But speaking of our upcoming nuptials seems to give him renewed vigor."

Less than three weeks now and we'd be forever joined in holy matrimony. Alrec wrapped his arms around me, drawing me into his embrace so he could kiss my temple.

My cheek. My earlobe. His mouth grew hungrier and more insistent as he worked his way down to my throat.

"I cannot wait for you to be mine," he murmured, hands drifting south.

I leaned into him, letting him hold me. But then my gaze landed on my new throne, and all I could think was how insignificant it looked compared to his. Yes, the king's power was greater than the queen's, but did it have to be so obvious? Was I to sit on that throne for the entirety of my reign and bow to his every whim? To be showered with lavish gowns and jewels but never be allowed to attend a council meeting? Never enter the war room? Never have a say?

I drew away, offering my husband-to-be a demure smile. "Thank you for the throne. It is truly beautiful."

"Not as beautiful as you," he returned, desire clouding his eyes.

When I stepped back and told him I'd see him at dinner, he frowned but quickly hid his disappointment behind one of his dazzling smiles. "I look forward to it."

I clutched my skirts, hurrying past Broderick. I needed to speak to my mother. Was I overreacting to this? Was this distinction simply one of those nonsensical human traditions that I needed to accept and move beyond? Unfortunately, she didn't answer at her door. So I made my way to Lowri's chamber instead.

"Lowri?" I knocked. "Are you here?" I needed to speak to someone—anyone—or else this nauseating feeling deep in the pit of my stomach was bound to get worse.

"Come in!"

The moment I opened the door, all I could smell was stale wine. Although much smaller than my own, Lowri's room still had a wide armoire filled with gowns and a white sleigh bed with two matching lockers that contrasted nicely with the blush-pink rosette wallpaper. I found my friend flicking through dresses, humming to herself, a half-empty bottle of faerie wine on the closest locker.

"Do I want to know what you're doing?" I asked, pleased to see her up and about.

"I need a new dress." Lowri snagged the bottle by the neck and brought it to her lips. When she'd finished, she returned it to the table and resumed her search.

"You bought four yesterday."

"Yes, but they won't be ready for weeks. And all of these are so—" She made a sound in the back of her throat.

"What's the occasion?" As far as I knew, the next big celebration would be my wedding day. A day I should be excited for, but instead I felt . . . nervous? Was that what this sick feeling was?

"The occasion," she said, "is dinner."

"Is there a special guest coming that I'm not aware of?" Alrec hadn't mentioned anything of the sort. Then again, if it didn't have to do with statues or tiny thrones, he probably didn't think it relevant.

"I want to look nice, that's all."

"You always look nice."

She harrumphed and took another drink. I sank onto the bed, leaning back against a mound of frilly throw pillows. "I take it you've recovered from yesterday's excitement?"

She paused her search long enough to sigh up at the ceiling. "Yesterday was a dream."

"A dream? Lowri, you spent most of the evening in tears." And she'd insisted on taking dinner in her room.

The scalloped hem of her navy skirts swayed along the carpet as she came toward me only to collapse onto the

mattress. "I was only crying because I was so torn over—"
She cut herself off, biting her lip.

"Over what?"

"It's just . . ." She sighed again, rising to her elbows to look at me, lavender hair spilling over her shoulders. "Did you see the way Prince Caiman swooped in and rescued me from that terrible man? He was so gallant."

First, he'd "rescued" both of us. Second, as far as I was concerned, there had been no swooping. Only Lowri losing her composure and Caiman offering comfort as if he weren't an evil wretch for once.

"One small act of kindness does not a hero make." Although if he truly hated the fae, surely he shouldn't have cared a whit about what anyone said about us. Perhaps it wasn't all fae he hated. Perhaps it was just me.

I found that harder to swallow than the alternative. What had I done to deserve his disdain? I thought back to the day we met. We'd escaped to the gardens, and I'd shown him a trick I'd learned from my father. We'd talked for hours and then he'd kissed me.

All right. Perhaps I'd kissed him. Not that it mattered since he didn't even remember. Either way, none of what had occurred that day had warranted what I'd overheard him saying to Alrec that same night.

She is a monster.

"I'm not so sure," Lowri said with a small, secret sort of smile.

I knew that smile. It was the same one she wore when she first met Lord Kerrington. "You cannot be serious. He's infuriating. Besides, I thought you were in love with Kerrington."

Lowri rolled off the bed, tore another gown from the armoire, wrinkled her freckled nose, and stuffed it back inside. "I told you, Kerrington was a mere distraction." She withdrew another gown, this one the color of a buttercup, but discarded it as well. "Besides, why should you be the only one with a prince on your arm?"

Surely she wasn't suggesting—

"Just think, if I married Alrec's brother, you and I would be sisters! Wouldn't that be a treat?"

For some reason, the idea of Lowri marrying Caiman sounded about as appealing as fish heads for supper. "The two of you wouldn't suit." She would drive him mad with her endless chatter, and he would reveal himself to be entirely heartless, breaking hers before nightfall.

"He may be all darkness and brooding now, but I am confident in my abilities to woo him into the light."

"Yes, but he is wretched."

"He is handsome," she countered, as if a nice face could excuse all manner of sins. "I have dreams too, you know. As much as I love being your lady-in-waiting, I would like a life of my own."

When she put it that way, who was I to deny her happiness? I'd found my prince. Didn't she deserve a chance to find hers?

Lowri yanked out a gorgeous black gown with a low-cut neckline that would enhance her curves. "This is it! This is the one." She spun in a circle, lavender curls bouncing.

I agreed that she would be a vision in the dress but couldn't find my smile.

6

____

ROISIN

I EXPLAINED TO LOWRI MY CONCERNS OVER THE THRONE AND she told me I was overreacting. That we should all be so lucky to have a prince who bought us gifts and gave us golden thrones. I felt so low by the time I left her chambers, the knots in my stomach had gotten worse.

I hadn't meant to sound ungrateful. I just . . . I don't know. None of it felt right.

When being indoors with my thoughts became too confining, I sought fresh air to clear my muddled mind. I passed through the solar and out onto the warm stone patio leading to the gardens.

The moment I was out of sight of the castle, I slipped out of my new shoes and tucked them beneath one of the hedges. Lush grass tickled my toes, grounding me.

Would Caiman buy Lowri slippers made of gold?

Not that I cared either way. She could pursue him all she wanted. Perhaps she could change his mind about the fae, since I clearly hadn't.

What was it about us that he despised so much? Or was it truly just me? I could ask Caiman outright what I'd done wrong, force him to tell me so that this festering wound I pretended wasn't there would finally heal. But who was to say he would give me an honest answer? And what would his response accomplish anyway? Sure, our relationship would be mended, but it wasn't as if it could take away four years of snide comments and hateful glares.

It didn't erase the other horrible things he'd done.

I made my way between hedges, past the rose trellis, to the lion-head fountains. A burbling stream snaked down the hill. Birds chirped as they flitted among the greenery.

The stream eventually widened into a large koi pond near the southern wall. A man in a white shirt and tan breeches sat on the arched bridge stretching over the water. It took me a moment to realize who it was.

Caiman, black hair pulled back from his angular face, booted feet swinging inches above a patch of lily pads.

I should've turned around. For some reason, I didn't feel like leaving. I felt like continuing to where the wicked prince sat, oblivious to the world with a book in his gloved hands, and asking him why he hated me.

Us, I mean. The fae. For Lowri. Wouldn't want her getting her hopes up only to have them dashed like mine.

The moment I set foot on the bridge, Caiman whirled, nearly dropping his book into the water. His wide, dark eyes gave away his surprise, which he quickly hid behind his trademark scowl.

"You're not wearing black," I said like a simpleton.

"Contrary to popular belief, the 'prince of darkness' does own clothes that are not black." He closed the book and set it aside. "And before you claim that I wore this as a disguise so that I could stalk you, might I point out that I was here first."

Fluffy clouds gathered over the horizon, painted shades

of pink and orange with the promise of evening. It'd be dinnertime soon. Would Lowri try to charm Caiman tonight? Would he enjoy it?

I sank onto a bowed wooden board next to him, my wide blue skirts brushing against his knee. "I'm glad I found you, actually."

"If I'd known you were looking, I would've found a better hiding place," he muttered.

He would not unsettle me. Not this time. "I'd like to thank you."

His dark brows came together.

"For helping Lowri yesterday," I clarified.

He dropped my gaze in favor of adjusting his gloves. "That pillock shouldn't have said that to her. To either of you."

"True. But he did. And you helped us when you didn't have to. For that, I am grateful. And I know she's grateful as well."

He twisted toward me, accidentally bumping his knee against mine. "If I hadn't gotten you away, something terrible could've happened."

"At least then you'd be free of me," I said with a humorless chuckle. Though all I really wanted to say was, *Why do you hate me?*

Caiman's black eyes narrowed before he angled himself back toward the pond. "I will never be free of you."

Before I could ask what that meant, he inquired after the maid I'd met in town.

"That girl's name is Falin," I said, "and she's a maid in your castle. Her mother passed a few months back, leaving her on her own to provide for three younger siblings. I gave her the purse because I thought it would help." She'd refused at first, but I'd insisted. Pride wouldn't put food on her table or buy clothes for her little brother and sisters. It wasn't fair that I had so much when others had so little. That may be the way of the world, but once I took my tiny throne, I was determined to do something about it.

I looked up to find Caiman's scowl replaced by an unreadable expression. Not a smile—heaven forbid the man smile at me. No, he looked confused. Was it any wonder? The idea of having compassion for others was probably a foreign concept to someone like him.

I shifted on the boards, my backside aching from the unforgiving wood. He still hadn't looked away. "Do you remember coming here when we first met?"

His dark brows pinched. "Did we?"

How could he forget so easily when the memory of that day had been burned into my mind? The day I'd found hope. The day I'd lost it. "I caught a fish with my bare hands."

"Surely I would recall something as impossible as that."

"You doubt it?"

The way his unnerving eyes raked from my burning cheeks down to my skirts and back again left my stomach quivering. "You do not appear to be the type of woman who would get her pretty dress dirty, let alone touch a slimy fish."

I knew I should let the past go. Leave it behind me where it belonged. But for some reason, I found myself climbing to my feet and tying my skirts between my knees the way I had four years ago. Caiman didn't say a word about the bits of grass clinging to my bare toes, only watched as I ducked beneath the wooden railing at the side of the bridge.

I smiled right at him and dropped into the frigid water with a splash. My feet sank deep into the muck at the bottom. Had it been this sticky and slimy the last time?

Water dampened my tied skirts, cooling my overwarm skin beneath.

Caiman shot to his feet, clutching the railing, his gaze sweeping from the path to the pond and back again. "Have you lost your mind? Someone may see you."

"Not if you keep your voice down," I shot back, bending forward and letting my fingers dip into the pond the way my father had taught me when I was small. The fish avoided me at first, an unfamiliar form in their tranquil home. I stayed perfectly still, allowing them to grow accustomed to my presence. One swam close, its tail tickling the back of my hand. Still I waited, knowing moving too hastily could spook them.

An orange fish with black smudges down its fins slipped lazily through the water. With a burst of fae speed, I caught the wriggling monster between my hands, heaving it into the air with a victorious smirk. It had to be at least two feet long. Caiman rolled his eyes. I considered throwing the beast at his insufferable head, but the fish hadn't done anything wrong and didn't deserve that sort of torment.

Something brushed my ankles. I knew it had to be another fish. It was only logical, after all. But in that moment, my mind conjured images of a heinous sea serpent, and I let out the most unladylike sound I'd ever made and jumped like a fool. The fish slipped, its tail flapping in my face, sending me careening backward.

My arms cartwheeled, but there was nothing to grab onto, and with no hope of catching myself, I sucked in a breath and braced for the icy splash. I managed to find my footing quickly, resurfacing with a sputter, only to find a scowly prince in soaked black breeches cursing as he reached for my hand.

"If you wanted to go for a bloomin' swim, you should've gone to the seaside. How do you plan on explaining this?"

"I'll just tell everyone you pushed me." I laughed, letting him help me upright.

He yanked me against him and clamped a sopping glove over my mouth. When I struggled, he only tightened his hold, hissing at me to be quiet as he dragged me beneath the bridge.

I thrashed and struggled, but he held firm. How could I have so easily forgotten Alrec's warnings about never letting myself be alone with him? All the hellish tales of Caiman's wickedness came flooding back as he forced me down until only my head peeked out of the water.

"Keep quiet. Someone's coming."

If I screamed, they could save me. I inhaled through my nose, prepared to shout for help.

"If anyone finds us like this, there will be hell to pay," he whispered. "For us both."

Realization struck like lightning.

He wasn't trying to attack me. He was trying to save me from the scandal of being caught unchaperoned with my fiancé's brother. The moment I began to relax, he let me go. I stared at the man next to me, hating that I noticed the way the drops of water ran down the column of his pale throat. The way they clung to his lips. That the humid air only enhanced the scent of sage and bergamot emanating from his skin. That I knew what he smelled like at all.

The water surrounding us turned glassy. I peered through the cobwebs on the underside of the bridge, listening to the unmistakeable sound of male voices as they came close. Voices I recognized. Alrec and Lord Kerrington chatting about a tennis match.

I tried not to think of what would have happened if Alrec had been the one to find us. Like me, he would've assumed the worst.

"You cannot tell him that I pushed you," Caiman whispered in earnest, his eyes wide and searching.

"I was only joking when I said that."

He didn't appear convinced.

"I will simply tell anyone who asks that I dropped something in the pond, and when I went to retrieve it, I slipped."

I expected him to leave, but instead he stepped closer, until I could feel the heat from his body warming the water between us. "About yesterday." He bit his lip, a war raging in his eyes. "I . . . I couldn't bear the thought of something happening to you."

I swallowed again and again, trying to get my heart out of my throat. "Why do you care?"

"I shouldn't. You're not my problem, you're Alrec's."

"I'm a problem, now, am I?"

"You were always a problem."

"How?" I whispered.

"Because there's only one of you and two of us." With that, Caiman ducked beneath the bridge and left me all alone.

7

CAIMAN

I PULLED ON MY LEATHER GLOVES, HURRYING ACROSS MY room to the door. My father's advisors had gathered to discuss the burgeoning conflict in the south. More enemy ships. More unveiled threats. More worries. More problems.

Only today, my father wouldn't be the one dealing with them. These issues, along with countless others, would fall to my brother's whims.

Alrec wasn't ready for this responsibility. Not because he was ill prepared but because his selfish arrogance wouldn't allow him to get out of his own way.

That's where I came in. Today was the day I would request an assignment as emissary. With my father's time drawing to an end, it wouldn't be long before I would be free of this castle. Of this utter torment wreaking havoc on my heart.

The moment Roisin had arrived at the pond, I should've gotten up and left. Instead, I'd stayed like some lovesick fool. And for what? To learn that she'd not only appreciated my pathetic attempt to keep herself and her Lady safe in the city but that she'd also gone out of her way to help a maid. As if I needed another reason to care when all I wanted was to hate her as thoroughly as she hated me.

I yanked open my door to find Roisin's friend on the other side. Lady Lowri hadn't stopped yammering all through dinner last night and had insisted on accompanying me to the drawing room afterward for a night cap, thanking me over and over for my "heroic display."

"If you're looking for Kerrington, his rooms are at the other end of the castle," I said, trying and failing to move past as she blocked my path.

She wrapped her cool, slender fingers around my wrist. To be so forward with a member of the royal family was unheard of. I tried not to recoil at her touch. "I was hoping to see you, actually."

"Why?"

"To thank you again. For what happened in the city."

"Think nothing of it."

Instead of moving or letting me go, she started blinking rapidly as she stared up at me.

"Do you have something in your eye?"

For some reason, that made her frown. "No."

Nothing more. Just "no" and more blinking.

And now a smile. Not a full smile but one that played on her mouth like she wasn't sure whether or not to use it.

"Right. Well, if that's all, I'm late for a meeting."

"It's not all, actually." She finally loosened her hold only to move closer, pinning me between herself and the door. I fumbled for the handle.

"I was wondering," she drawled, "if you'd like to accompany me to dinner this evening?"

"Why?"

The giggling woman smacked my arm, said she'd meet

me in the hallway at half seven, and left before I could turn her down.

Women. If only they came with some sort of handbook.

Nothing they did made any bloomin' sense.

Roisin, for example. From the way she treated me, I'd been convinced she was as heartless as my brother. Then she not only put herself at risk to speak to that maid but also gave her money.

Roisin had a heart . . . and she'd given it to the worst person I knew.

I hurried a suspiciously empty hall, rounding the corner and coming to a skidding halt.

A familiar blond head bent over a feminine frame, tucked into one of the many alcoves along the window-lined breezeway. Just what I wanted to see after dreaming all night about the one woman I could never have.

I was about to turn around until I saw a lock of black hair fall over the woman's shoulder.

Had my brother lost his mind? What if someone else had stumbled upon him snogging a blasted courtier in the bloomin' hallway? What if it had been Roisin? She'd never forgive him. Maybe she'd realize the mistake she made and—

I wiped the smile from my face.

That ship had long since sailed. I was on a new mission now. One that required my brother's cooperation.

Bite your tongue.

Say nothing.

Move along.

Alrec glanced over his shoulder, visibly balking when he saw me. The woman had the decency to blush before she ran past in a swish of skirts and sickly-sweet perfume.

Alrec dabbed at the rouge stains on his lips with a

golden handkerchief before stuffing it away in his waistcoat pocket and straightening his untucked shirt. "Fine weather we're having, wouldn't you say?"

"It is," I clipped, managing to keep the extent of my disdain from showing on my face. No point in fighting when Alrec always won.

My teeth rattled when he clapped me on the shoulder. "There's a good man."

I shrugged him off, continuing on my way to the door down the hall, now most assuredly late. No one would judge my brother; he was to be king, after all. The same leniency did not extend to me.

As I had feared, by the time we reached the privy council chambers, the twelve members were already seated around the long mahogany table strewn with maps and missives, glaring at the clock over the mantle.

"It is kind of you to decide to join us, Prince Caiman," Lord Devon said from the top of the table, two seats down from my father's empty place at its head. Beside him, his son Kerrington smirked. The two shared the same red hair, but that's where the similarities ended.

When the door opened behind me, everyone shot to their feet, chairs scraping as they bowed to their soon-to-be king. "Prince Alrec, it is a relief to see you looking so fit and healthy this day," Lord Devon said, watching with wide eyes as my brother took our father's throne.

A throne that should've been left vacant out of deference to the king.

"Thank you, Lord Devon." Alrec gave everyone a dismissive wave. "You may be seated."

The rest of the men took their seats. I slid into the chair to my brother's left, where I'd sat since I was a boy. Alrec's usual chair, to our father's right, remained empty.

Alrec collected a stack of parchments from the table, shuffling through the pages without reading them. "What's the first order of business today?"

Lord Devon cleared his throat. "Three more ships have been spotted in the southern bay. That makes seven in total, far too many to be considered a peaceful endeavor."

The map spread wide outlined all our territories, including the neighboring island of Airren and the northern island of Alba. On the right side of the map, the continent jutted out, marking the beginning of King Tarren's territory.

Alrec dropped the missives to tent his fingers beneath his chin. I'd always envied the beard he'd had since he'd turned sixteen. At nineteen, my face was still as smooth as a babe's. I had precisely three chin hairs. Still, I shaved twice a week in the hopes of encouraging more.

"It sounds to me as though we need a show of force to let King Tarren know this sort of behavior will not be tolerated under my rule."

The advisors exchanged glances, the weight of Alrec's words leaving a bitter, acidic tang in the air.

Lord Devon was the only man to speak up. "With all due respect, your highness, such a show of force may provoke an attack. Wouldn't it be more advisable to send an emissary to the continent to speak with the king first? Your brother, perhaps?"

My throat dried up at his words. As much as it warmed me to know Lord Devon believed I would be a good man for the position, it was far too early in this meeting to suggest such a thing. I hadn't even made my case.

"My brother?" Alrec scoffed. "Surely you jest. Sending someone so weak would only make us appear weak in return."

Every ounce of hope in my being died. My one and only chance to escape, squandered. What now? Was I to remain in this castle for the rest of my days, watching the woman I loved—

I shook my head, dispelling the traitorous thought. Was I to watch Alrec run this kingdom into the ground and start a bloomin' war just so that he could have another accomplishment to gloat about in years to come?

Kerrington nodded emphatically. "An excellent point, Prince Alrec. We wouldn't want our enemies to think us a bunch of twiddling twats, too weak to defend our borders."

I swallowed the acid on my tongue. Being called a "twiddling twat" was actually a fairly good put-down coming from a brainless weasel. "If not a twiddling twat such as myself, who would you suggest as emissary?"

Kerrington's pointed chin thrust forward so he could look down his nose at me. "It would be my honor to serve my kingdom in such a way."

No no no. Kerrington never showed interest in anything. Why the hell did he have to be interested in this? If Alrec had to choose between the two of us, there'd be no contest.

Alrec's head tilted as he considered. "I see no point in sending an emissary to speak with a man clearly posturing in our territory."

"The waters belong to no nation," I reminded him. Technically, King Tarren could float all of his ships just off our shores and there was nothing we could do about it.

"That may be the old way, *little* brother, but I see this as a clear act of aggression, and it will not be tolerated. I say we send a fleet to the bay and meet them with force."

The whispers in the chamber turned to murmurs of discontent. The fool wasn't even king yet and, if their worried looks were any indication, their support already wavered.

I thought back to that day in the city when I should've spoken up about the number of guards but hadn't. Preventing war was more important than whatever punishment my brother was bound to inflict. "Do we know if Iodale's king is having the same problem?" I asked Devon.

"We haven't heard." Lord Devon glanced at the men shaking their heads for confirmation. "I can draft a letter if your highness wishes it."

Although the question had been directed at me, Alrec was the one to answer. "No, I do not wish it. What happens in Iodale is their own problem. What's happening in the bay is ours."

"If this confrontation is to end in war, we will need alliances," said Lord Devon.

Alrec couldn't be serious. As the heir to the throne, he should know better than anyone that forming alliances was one of the first steps in warfare. We may have been a large island, but we were still an island. What hope did we have of winning a war against a nation with unlimited access to resources when ours could be cut off with a few well-placed ships?

Not to mention, all of our closest allies were islands as well. And Iodale was his betrothed's home country. Wouldn't he want to protect their people as well as our own?

"Fine," Alrec ground out, splaying his hands atop the missives. "I will allow you to write to the King of Iodale. But we will also send ships with cannons and munitions to the bay. It will appease the lords living close by *and* show Tarren we aren't to be trifled with."

Lord Devon bowed his head. "As you wish, your highness."

"Now, let's get on to the next order of business." Alrec's grin left my heart sinking. "My coronation."

When the discussion around Alrec's coronation lasted twice as long as the discussion of an impending war, that was all the confirmation I needed that our country was doomed. He'd always been a curse in my life, one-upping me at every turn, but I refused to let him curse this kingdom.

Alrec could plan his ridiculously lavish coronation ceremony. Let him have the cakes and crown and dancers and jesters and choruses of people singing his praises. His distraction would give me a chance to fix the situation in the south.

Eventually, he grew bored of the discussions and dismissed everyone like they were a nuisance. When I stood to join them, he told me to sit back down. I remained standing behind my chair.

"I said *sit!*" Alrec roared, banging his fists on the table like a petulant child impatient for dinner.

As much as it killed me to do so, I sank back onto the hard wooden chair.

He leaned forward, pointing a thick finger at my face. "If you ever make me look like a fool in front of my advisors again—"

"Sorry, but you did that all by yourself."

"Interrupt me once more, and I will have you thrown into the dungeon. Do you hear me, Caiman?"

"But with me dead, who would you blame for all your missteps?" It was dangerous, pushing him when he was in this form, but I was so far beyond caring.

"You dare speak that way to your king?"

"Bedwyr is my king."

"Not for long. And when I am on the throne, I will make your life hell."

How would that be any different from the last nineteen years? What could he do to me that hadn't already been done? He'd thrown me into a fire, broken my limbs and nose, bruised my ribs more times than I cared to count, and yet somehow managed to turn everything around and make it look as though I'd deserved the thrashings. And now he'd stolen the future I'd planned for myself, all because he thought I was too weak. "Why not just send me away and be done with it? Let me serve as emissary and I will be out of your hair for good."

He stilled, and for a moment, I believed I had gotten through to him.

Then he sneered. "I have a better idea. This war *will* happen. When I win, I will put you in charge of my statue. And you will erect it somewhere you will see it every single day of your life."

"Why must you make everything into some sort of competition? Can't you see you've already won? You've won, and I've lost. Now, I'm begging you to think this through. Your decision will cost others their lives. You can still be a decent king. Start by setting a good example for your people instead of disappointing them from the moment your arse lands on our father's throne."

His narrowed eyes widened. "You think winning a war would be a disappointment? I will be revered as a god. They will write songs commemorating my victory."

"Or they'll curse your name for sending them out to fight while you hide inside these walls like a coward. If you sent me as emissary—"

He lunged, catching me by the collar. Spittle hit my face

when he growled, "After the way you've questioned my authority in front of everyone? I'd sooner send my wife."

He let me go with a shove, and I fell back against my chair, gasping and massaging my neck. "She's your betrothed, not your wife."

He blinked at me once. Twice. "That's what this is about, isn't it?" he said slowly. "Even after all these years, you still cannot stand the fact that she chose me."

"She didn't choose you. She chose to be queen."

Alrec's face went as red as his overcoat.

Dammit. I'd pushed him too far. I'd be lucky if I only ended up in the dungeon for the week.

"Is that what you think?"

If I was to be sent to the dungeon, I may as well earn it. "I think you are weak of mind and character. I think you are unfit to sit on our father's throne. I think you will run this kingdom into the ground. And I think Roisin chose wrong."

Alrec's hand fell to the pommel of the short sword he wore at his waist.

What was he going to do? Kill me? He wouldn't dare. Except the way he drew his sword, with deliberate slowness, and aimed it at my chest said differently. Something moved in the corner of my eye. Broderick emerged from between two suits of armor, his hand on the hilt of his weapon.

Alrec's twisted smile faltered for a split second before he pressed the tip of his blade against my hammering heart. Every ounce of his hatred, I returned tenfold. It hummed in my veins. Lived on my tongue. "Do it. You know you want to."

"And put you out of your misery? I think not." Sneering, he returned his sword to its sheath. "Instead, I will accompany my soldiers to the bay and lead them into battle while you hide inside these walls 'like a coward.'"

Had he lost his mind? "You can't—"

"All the while, I will be thinking on your punishment for this defiance. When I return, you will be sorry you ever stood against me."

He stood and stalked from the room. Broderick gave me one final glance before following my brother into the hallway.

Alrec was going to start a war just to spite me?

Good god, what had I done?

8

ROISIN

A petal-scented breeze caught the blue satin ribbon in my hair, twisting and tugging, mimicking the way my heart felt in my chest. In the distance, bees buzzed and horses knickered.

"I will miss you every moment of every day that I am gone," Alrec whispered, pressing a warm kiss to my forehead.

A mass of soldiers waited at his back, standing at attention in orderly lines. The gold buttons on their red coats glinted in the blinding sun. Lord Devon and Kerrington remained with the other advisors next to the castle stairs. Lowri's violet hair peeked from behind them as she bobbed up and down, no doubt standing on her tiptoes to see over the crowd. Instead of coming to see them off, my mother had chosen to remain inside with the king.

"Are you certain you must go?" With his father so unwell, surely someone could travel to Southbay in his stead. What about Caiman? Alrec's brother scowled from the castle's main doorway, cloaked in shadows. "Why not send your brother?"

Alrec's face turned as red as his coat; a vein in his forehead bulged. "Do not say that traitor's name. Promise me you will not so much as speak to him while I am away."

"We share the same dinner table every night. Am I to ignore him completely?"

He brushed a tendril of hair from my cheek. "You know what he's like. The things he's done. I am only concerned for your safety."

One of the officers shouted from among the ranks, announcing the army's imminent departure and saving me from having to respond.

Alrec cupped my face, pressing his forehead to mine. "I have left a surprise for you for each day until I return."

Alrec and his surprises. I managed a laugh despite the heaviness swelling inside my heart. "Be safe. The kingdom needs you. I need you."

"I will," he promised.

I watched him mount his horse, already counting the hours until he returned.

The robin's-egg blue walls in my bed chamber had been edged in pure gold leaf. My bed's scrolled headboard resembled the crest of a wave, enriched with more gold. But the most beautiful piece had to be the chandelier dangling from the coffered ceiling. At night, I would lie awake and stare at the moonlight playing on the crystals like rambunctious stars.

My mother hummed from the adjoining sitting room, likely reading on the balcony. A soft breeze flowed through the open window, marking another fine day in Vellana.

Alrec had left for Southbay six days ago. He'd sworn he

would be home well in time for the wedding. We still had four days before we would walk down the aisle in the castle's small chapel. Even so, I stared out the window toward the castle gates, growing more anxious with every moment that passed, searching for a handsome prince riding a white horse.

Perhaps Lowri and I could go for a ride this afternoon to take my mind off things. My toes flexed on the cream and blue carpet. Then again, if I went for a ride, I'd be expected to put on stockings and shoes. The stockings were bearable, but I'd despised shoes ever since I was a girl. My mother used to have to bribe me with sweets to put them on.

Lowri withdrew yet another fabulous gown from the oversized armoire. "He is most kind. And have you seen his eyes?"

Of course I'd seen Caiman's eyes. They were in his head. She hadn't stopped swooning over the evil prince since she'd set her sights on him. "He's not the man you think he is."

"How would you know? You haven't spent any time at all in his company. He doesn't say much, but I imagine it won't be long until he announces his intentions."

I sat up straighter, clutching my skirts. "He is courting you?"

"Not officially. But I have made my desire plain."

"How plain? Lowri, you need to be careful."

The dress's chiffon skirts gently swished as she swung it toward me. "This one is absolutely divine."

"Yes, it's gorgeous. But Lowri—"

"Gorgeous? You will be a vision." Lowri hooked the hanger on the edge of the oversized gilt-framed mirror standing against the wall.

I rose to my feet, needing to explain to her Caiman's

dark past so that she would realize she was far better off pursuing someone else.

A woman's blood-curdling scream shot through the open window.

Lowri and I rushed to where the lace curtains fluttered. In the courtyard below, a swarm of soldiers in red uniforms pushed through the gates. Women toting children and carrying baskets of laundry screamed and shouted when three of the men collapsed onto the cobblestones. More men in soiled breeches and bloodied shirts hauled in bodies, helping their fellow comrades limp to the castle steps.

My mother burst into the room, her silver hair flying behind her.

Fear and terror settled in my stomach next to the pear tarts we'd eaten for our tea. "What's happened?"

"I don't know. But we must hurry. We need to help if we can."

I didn't bother throwing on shoes, following my mother's billowing skirts into the hallway with Lowri close at my heels. Servants and guards poured from rooms, all headed in the same direction. A tall, balding man in a baldric and leather pants barked orders at the doors, calling for water and towels, needles and thread.

When I hit the top of the steps leading down to the courtyard, the roaring of my heart in my ears stilled. The stench of gunpowder and coppery tang of blood washed over me like a rogue wave. There were bodies everywhere. Soldiers with bloody head wounds, gashes in their sides, missing limbs.

Someone grabbed my arms. "Roisin, look at me." My mother's voice was as sharp as a blade. "Heal as many as you can. If your magic is blocked, move on. Do you understand?" She squeezed my arms to the point of pain. "Roisin!"

"I understand."

She took off, racing toward a man with the side of his face burned away. Lowri appeared frozen on the stairs, taking in the horror with wide, terrified eyes. I shouted for her to fetch a bucket of water. She spun toward the door and disappeared.

Some of the men didn't seem to have sustained too much damage. I bypassed them in favor of a man leading another with a crude bandage wrapped in a torniquet around his thigh. "Set him down here," I told the man holding him upright. Once the wounded soldier had been laid onto the sun-warmed stones, Lowri appeared, shoving a towel beneath his head.

Untying the bandage could bring about more bleeding, but since the blood appeared to be dry, I assumed the wound had clotted. "I need to get to his leg."

The man withdrew a dagger from his belt, cutting the breeches away, revealing deep purple bruises extending from beneath the bandages. I pressed my hands to the exposed skin, closed my eyes, and tried to focus on sending my magic, but there was too much noise and mayhem.

The air reeked of blood and what if I couldn't save him and—

I could do this.

I *would* do this.

After three deep breaths, heat collected in my chest, streaming down my arms toward my hands and passing into the man's leg. It felt as though I was throwing it into a void, filling the emptiness with all I had, and yet it wasn't working. I gave more and more, sweat collecting on my brow. I felt the man's need begin to wane. When I opened my eyes, the color had returned to his face.

"He should be all right," I assured his friend before standing on wobbly legs and moving on to the next soldier, a man who looked as if someone had hacked at his shoulder with a saw. Before I closed my eyes, I saw a figure in all black sprinting down the stairs, heading for the heart of the mele.

Prince Caiman vanished into the crowd while Lord Kerrington stood on the bottom step, his face an unhealthy shade of green. I forced them both from my mind, closing my eyes and reaching for my magic, hating how thin it felt as I pushed it toward the wounded soldier. Once he'd been healed, I went to the next man. And the next, and the next, Lowri at my side, offering assistance where she could.

"Milady, please," a man begged, waving frantically at me from where he knelt by a soldier with pain-glazed eyes. "Please help 'im. He's my best mate. Please."

My knees cracked against the cobblestones when I fell to his side, sending pain shooting through my legs. "Where was he struck?"

The man tugged up his friend's shirt, revealing purple and blue bruises across his abdomen. Lowri gasped, clutching her throat. "What happened to him?"

"Cannon fire, milady."

"Cannon fire? Where?" I hadn't heard any cannon fire, and my fae ears could hear better than most.

"In Southbay."

The world suddenly tilted on its side, forcing me to clutch the ground to keep from falling into a chasm of utter hopelessness.

Alrec had gone to Southbay. What if he was here? I had to check. I had to find him. When I went to stand, the man caught my hand, his own fingers bandaged and bloody. "Please, milady. Please don't leave 'im."

One more. One more man, then I'd search for my prince.

As with the others, I closed my eyes, directed my healing magic, waited and . . .

Blocked.

I tried and tried and tried, but nothing I did made a difference. The man was dying, and there was nothing I could do to stop it.

That isn't true.

I could give my immortal life in exchange for his. The man's friend looked at me with such hope. Hope I was about to steal away. "I'm . . . I'm so sorry. There's nothing I can do."

The soldier's eyes filled with tears. His head started to shake. "No . . . No . . ." He took his friend's hand, murmuring words of quiet reassurance.

"Stay with him," I told Lowri, her eyes as watery as my own. "Make him comfortable."

When I stood, my spinning head left me stumbling until an arm snaked around my waist, keeping me from collapsing. The rich scent of sage and bergamot teased my senses. I knew who held me without having to turn.

"I tried to save him." My voice trembled as I listened to the dying man's last rattling breaths with tears streaming down my cheeks. "I tried, but he was . . ."

"It's not your fault," Caiman said. "You need rest."

How could I rest when there were still at least thirty men who needed tending? The physician I'd met in the king's suite was there, and my mother darted from one man to the next, healing what appeared to be the worst cases. If I were stronger, perhaps I could've saved him.

"I can't. These men were in Southbay. With Alrec."

"I know. None of them have seen my brother."

That had to be a good sign, right? That he wasn't among the wounded. He must be out there, bringing more men back to the castle.

I searched the faces for one I recognized. As much as I wanted to help the others, I had to conserve the rest of my magic in case Alrec needed me. I wouldn't fail him the way I had failed the last man, now staring blankly toward the cloudless sky.

A tall soldier in blackened livery stumbled among the fallen men, clutching his side.

My heart swelled with hope. "Is that . . . ?"

"Broderick," Caiman finished, his hand at my waist tightening.

I would've given out about the way he held me, except without him I wasn't sure I'd be able to stand. Together, we started for Broderick. The closer we drew, the more I panicked. He appeared to be alone. He was never alone. He was Alrec's shadow. Where was my fiancé?

When the guard saw us approaching, he grimaced.

"Where is he?" Caiman demanded.

Broderick's dark eyes shuttered. "Prince Alrec," he choked, drawing in a rasping breath and clutching his bleeding side, "is dead."

9

CAIMAN

I'D BATHED THRICE SINCE THE CHAOS IN THE COURTYARD, and yet I still felt blood on my hands. Three days had passed, but I didn't think I'd ever feel clean again. My brother's foolish arrogance had cost twenty-seven men their lives. Wives made widows. Children left fatherless. And for what? So he could prove to me that he was invincible?

Alrec may have been the one to issue the order, but he wouldn't have been in Southbay if I hadn't pushed him to the limit. What had I been thinking? I knew he would never back down from a challenge. And now he was gone.

"I don't understand," my father kept muttering, blank eyes searching the shadowed ceiling for answers. "He is to be king. He is the king . . ."

The king didn't fight his own battles. He had soldiers do it for him. As the useless second son, it should've been my responsibility to serve in the army, but my physical ailments as a child had kept me from that life.

It should've been me.

Alrec had a kingdom who loved him. And Roisin . . .

She hadn't left her chambers in days.

In the courtyard, she hadn't balked at the blood staining her hands or bare feet, ruining her fine blue gown. She'd been brilliant, healing wounded men as if they were her own people, stepping seamlessly into the role of the queen I always hoped she could be.

And then Broderick had given us the devastating news.

I'd refused to believe it, ordering Lord Devon to have fresh troops sent to Southbay to scour the coast for any sign of my brother. Of the twenty-seven men killed, seven of them had been lost at sea. Seven bodies never recovered, my brother's among them.

Broderick had left the infirmary earlier this morning, lucky to be alive. If it weren't for Lady Seren's healing magic, his fate would've been the same as—

Dammit.

I dropped my head into my hands. Alrec couldn't be dead. He couldn't.

My father turned to me, a rare moment of clarity crossing his sunken eyes as he took my hand, his grip surprisingly strong for a man at death's door. His rattling inhale left me sinking even lower. "You must honor the betrothal contract."

"Father, you're not thinking straight." It must be the morphine talking. Roisin could go back to Iodale and find some other wealthy lord to marry.

"I made a promise to Lady Seren that her daughter would wed my son. I swore . . . I swore it to the fae." My father struggled to draw himself upright against the dark headboard. I put a hand on his shoulder to keep him abed. Now, more than ever, he needed to conserve what little strength he had. I couldn't lose him too. "You are the only son I have left."

The back-up.

The contingency.

The spare.

"To break the betrothal would bring dishonor to this household. Could bring war back to our shores. I am still your king." His eyes fell closed, and he whispered, "Your duty is to honor the contract."

I don't know how long I sat there staring, my world falling apart once again. To him, this was a business arrangement, pure and simple. To me, it wasn't.

This was my life. Roisin's life. Tying the two of us together would only end in disaster. With my brother gone, the throne—and its mountain of responsibilities—would fall to me.

Wasn't that enough?

As king, I'd be expected to marry, but it didn't have to be her. It could be someone else—anyone else.

Dammit. I didn't want to be king.

When my father began to snore, I eased off the mattress, careful not to disturb him. Perhaps Lady Seren had been wrong and he'd recover, hold the throne for another decade or two. Then I'd have some time to prepare. To figure things out.

I stalked out of his bedroom into the privy chamber, knowing such notions were a fantasy. My father wouldn't last a decade. I'd be lucky if he lasted the month.

I knew for a fact that Roisin would rather carve out my heart than have me as her husband. Perhaps she would. It was no less than I deserved after what had happened to Alrec.

Broderick stepped out of an alcove, and I nearly rammed into the man. I'd never get used to the way he moved, silent as a bloomin' wraith. At times it was like he appeared out of thin air. Now that my brother was gone, he'd been assigned to me. I didn't need a blasted guard. I wanted to be left alone.

He followed me through the king's study and into the hallway.

Did Roisin know that she was expected to honor the contract? If not, someone should tell her. I was the last person she'd want to see. Still, we needed to discuss what was to happen now that everything had changed.

What should I say?

First, I needed to apologize for this mess. Why the hell had I pushed Alrec that day? Why hadn't I kept my mouth shut? Bitten my tongue? Insisted he drive his sword through my worthless heart?

"Do you have much experience with women?" I asked, turning to face my guard.

Broderick's eyes widened, and he looked around. "Sire?"

"Women. What do they like?"

Redness crept from his high collar to his ears. "I . . . um . . . Well . . ." He cleared his throat. "I'm not sure I under-stand the question."

I glanced down the hall toward Roisin's room. "I need to speak to Lady Roisin. But I'm probably the last person she wants to talk to." Bloody hell, this was a disaster. "Do you have any ideas on how to make this easier?"

Broderick blew out a breath. "Oh, right. Ah . . . my mother used to like when I brought her flowers."

Flowers. Of course. I would get Roisin some flowers. I started for the gardens, my new guard close behind. Five minutes later, we stepped onto the sandstone patio surrounded by raised beds.

Why were there so many to choose from? Red ones, blue ones, yellow ones . . . Which would Roisin like best? I glanced at Broderick. "Any ideas?"

"Not one."

The pink ones looked nice. And they reminded me of her cheeks when she blushed. I grabbed a handful, tearing them out by the stems and getting the roots as well. Dirt tumbled all over my boots. Broderick reached into the sheath at his belt and withdrew a dagger, cutting the stems at the base.

"Thank you, Broderick."

"You're welcome, your highness."

I paused in the doorway to Roisin's chambers. It was just a door. Nothing to be scared of. All I had to do was knock. Just raise my fist and give it a swift *one, two*.

My hand balled into a fist and . . . I couldn't do it.

What the hell was I going to say to her, anyway? *Here, take these flowers. By the way, sorry I'm responsible for your fiancé's death. How about you marry me instead?*

Could you imagine? Maybe I should come back tomorrow, once I'd had more time to prepare.

I turned to leave; Broderick blocked my exit. Before I could tell him to get out of the way, the bastard leaned forward and rapped on the door.

The door flew open, and Roisin's mother appeared with a demure smile. "Prince Caiman. What a pleasant surprise." Her gaze dropped to the pathetic heap of flowers strangled in my fist, and a ghost of a smile crossed her lips.

"Is your . . . ah . . . daughter here?" I managed through my tight throat. "I would like to speak with her."

"She is. Come in." She stepped aside, opening the door wider. "I'll get Roisin now." Her skirts swirled as she turned for the adjoining bedchambers. My heart beat wildly in my chest.

"I'm not going out there," Roisin hissed a moment later, "and you cannot make me."

"He is to be your husband. You need to speak with him."

"I'd rather die than marry that evil wretch."

"Keep your voice down. Do you want him to hear you?"

"As if I care. You know what? I've changed my mind. I *will* speak to him, so I can tell him to his face that he is a—"

A door slammed. Lady Seren came out, her smile tight and shoulders rigid. "I'm afraid my daughter is feeling unwell at the moment. It has been a trying week for us all. Perhaps you could call back later when she is feeling better?"

What other choice did I have? "You might tell her that I . . . ah . . . I hope she feels better soon. Good day, Lady Seren." My shoulders fell as I started for the exit. Time to deal with the rest of the disaster that had become my life. Lord Devon wanted to meet to discuss news from the Black City and—

"Prince Caiman?"

I stilled halfway to the door. Before I could turn, Roisin's mother wrapped me in a vanilla-scented embrace. When was the last time someone had hugged me?

My mother. She'd hugged me that fateful morning. Told me she loved me.

When I'd returned to her chambers for lunch, I'd found her on the floor.

My throat closed as the tears came. No matter how many times I swallowed, the pain refused to ease.

When Lady Seren drew away, she offered a sad smile. "It is sometimes difficult to bring ourselves from our own grief to acknowledge someone else's. My daughter may have lost her betrothed, but you lost your brother. And for that, I am so dreadfully sorry."

Alrec was no more my brother than Broderick. Still, I accepted the gesture with a nod and continued into the hall.

All of this was such a bloomin' mess. A disaster. *Dammit.*

I launched the forgotten flowers against the wall. I'd never wanted any of this. My gaze snagged on Roisin's door. That wasn't entirely true, was it? I may have wanted her, but not by default or at Alrec's expense. I'd wanted her to choose me.

Broderick began collecting the flowers, making me feel like a bold child. "I'll take care of it," I told him, dropping to my knees to help pick them up. There was no sense in the staff having to come by and do it either. I made the mess and was perfectly capable of cleaning up after myself.

He handed me the broken stems with a stern frown. The same one my father used to wear when I'd throw a fit over Alrec beating me at one thing or another. A game. A race. A fight.

"Sometimes my temper gets the better of me," I confessed.

Broderick's eyebrows arched. "Is that so? Because I have never seen a man with more restraint."

"How can you say that when you know the truth?" That I'd baited Alrec. Taunted him into doing something so foolish.

"I can say it *because* I know the truth."

He was wrong. A better man would've held his tongue until we'd both calmed down and spoken rationally. A better man would've done anything to stop his brother from charging off to his own death.

Again, I glanced at the door, wishing there was some way to make this better.

"Give her time," Broderick said. "She will come around."

Would she? For some reason, she had loved my brother. Love didn't just go away overnight. "She mourns a man who never existed." If Roisin knew the truth about the way he delighted in torture and dallied with other women, the terrible things he'd done, she would've been thanking her lucky stars to be rid of him.

Offering me a hand, Broderick sighed and said, "He existed to her."

10

ROISIN

Rain splattered against the chapel's slate roof, and all I could think was, "Even the sky is crying." On any other day it would've been calming, lulling me back to sleep. Not today. The dark clouds and rain were a sign of the darkness that had infiltrated my future. I had begged and pleaded with the stars over my fate. Mother had said this was my destiny, that taking the throne of Vellana was bigger than me, than any of us. It would signify peace between humans and fae, the end of hundreds of years of animosity and prejudice held by those in power.

I was meant to be marrying Alrec in my ivory silk gown and cathedral veil that stretched the length of the chapel's red and gold carpet. I was meant to be walking toward a man with golden hair matching the golden crown on his head, not a devil with black hair, blacker eyes, and the blackest soul. A devil who would soon be king by the look of his father propped up beneath a mound of fur blankets on the front pew.

I could protest.

I could outright refuse.

I could hurtle straight for the door and escape the noose closing around my neck.

Except I would never consider bringing such shame to my mother. This union symbolized so much more than the marriage of two people who despised each other.

This was the dawn of a new age.

Unfortunately, the price of that new age was my life and my happiness.

In front of me, Lowri walked in time to the music played by the stringed quartet tucked beneath a rosette window. She had been unusually quiet ever since she learned I was to marry Caiman.

I didn't have the words to make her feel better.

I was too empty.

Dark pews lined either side of the aisle, filled with noblemen and their wives. Although invitations had been extended to our friends and relatives living in Iodale, I saw no familiar faces or pointed ears.

A massive pipe organ rose like some metallic beast at Caiman's back. Broderick kept his post next to the rear exit. On the opposite side sat a gilt-framed portrait of a young, majestic Alrec from his funeral two days earlier.

In the four weeks since the attack in the bay, I'd kept hold of the hope that Alrec had somehow survived. Each time a search party returned empty handed, that hope dwindled until only a thread remained. On the day we buried an empty casket, that final thread had snapped.

The veil I wore concealed the tears tumbling down my cheeks as my heart clattered against my ribcage. My feet ached inside the golden slippers Alrec had gifted me, itching to turn back toward the exit. I clutched the bouquet of blush-colored roses until my fingers cramped.

A death march. That's what this was. Signifying the end of my life as I knew it.

If I focused solely on the bright red of Caiman's fitted coat, I could pretend he was Alrec. After what felt like forever yet no time at all, I reached the end of the aisle. When Caiman made to lift my veil, I stepped back. His gloved hands fell to his sides. I imagined his eyes narrowed but didn't glance up from the petal-strewn runner to check.

"Dearly beloved, we are gathered here today . . ." The priest's words jumbled into a dull hum.

I promised Caiman things that belonged to his brother.

My heart.

My faithfulness.

My love.

When he repeated the vows in his low timbre, chills snaked down my bare arms and foreboding settled in my core. I didn't look at him until the priest pronounced us husband and wife and said that the prince could kiss his bride.

This time, I knew better than to shrink away when two gloved hands lifted my veil.

Tears clouded my vision, but I refused to let him see me cry. Caiman leaned forward and pressed a kiss to my cheek.

For a moment, I remembered the way his lips had felt that day four years ago. We'd both been so bumbling and awkward, I'd ended up in a fit of giggles.

She's a monster.

Those words were all I could hear as he straightened and offered me his arm. I forced myself to take it, the sleeve of his coat soft beneath my fingertips. A riotous cheer lifted as we turned to face the eager crowd. My mother dabbed at her cheeks from where she sat next to the king, a comforting hand over his limp one. When we reached the door, two servants waited with wide umbrellas to stave off the rain. The red carpet sloshed beneath my slippers as we took the short walk through the courtyard to the castle.

Caiman didn't bother trying to make small talk, but I dared a glance at him from beneath my lashes. Dark, slashing brows. Straight, regal nose. High, sharp cheek-bones. Slightly pointed chin. Full lips—My stomach fluttered.

Traitor.

That's what I was.

A traitor to true love.

What followed was a blur of food and drink, dancing and well-wishes. Lowri stayed at my side for all of it, feeding me glass after glass of faerie wine.

At some point late in the night, the king lifted his goblet with a trembling hand and clinked his spoon against it until the raucous laughter and conversations quieted. "Our dearest friends and family, we thank you all for braving the rain today to help us celebrate this momentous occasion." He turned, his sunken eyes crinkling with his smile. "Roisin, you are a rare beauty indeed, a vision of poise and grace. My son—" The king's voice broke. "My son is a lucky man."

I felt Caiman's eyes on me but didn't dare look toward him, focusing instead on the way his father blinked back tears.

"Caiman, I am proud of the man you have become, someone who puts duty and kingdom above all else."

Caiman shifted on his chair.

The king raised his goblet toward the glittering chande-lier. "To Prince Caiman and Princess Roisin."

The rest of the crowd mimicked the movement, repeating after him.

I put the first part out of my mind and focused on the second. I was now a princess, something every little girl dreamed of at least once in her life. If only the new title hadn't come with such heavy burdens.

Caiman raised his glass, then took a small sip before setting it aside.

I guzzled what was left of mine. Lowri had another one waiting for me.

"I'm not sure I can stomach it," I confessed, glaring at the greenish-yellow liquid as it sloshed around in my glass.

"Do you really want to remember today? I know I certainly don't," she muttered.

I didn't want to remember anything either. Past, present, or future. The gold band on my finger felt heavy. Why was it so heavy? My hair felt heavy too. And my shoes. I should probably take them off. My shoes, not my hair. I giggled to myself.

Lowri forced the glass stem between my fingers before adjusting the slipping neckline on my wedding dress.

Caiman glanced sidelong at me, raising an arrogant brow. By the time I finished, my face felt all tingly, and there wasn't one Caiman but two. And both of them were scowling at me as he offered his gloved hand. What was he doing that for? I didn't want to hold his hand. Why did he wear those silly gloves anyway?

The twin Caimans cleared their throats. "It is customary for a husband to dance with his wife at the wedding," he said in that low voice of his. I hated that it made my heart clench. I hated everything about him. His irritatingly handsome face. His obnoxiously dark eyes. His too-full lips.

One dance. That was all. Then I could stumble away from the festivities and hide in my chambers.

"Fine." I put my hand in his, my knees nearly giving out

when I pushed from the chair. "Let's get this over with." Hopefully no one noticed my abandoned shoes beneath the dining table. It probably didn't offer the best impression to be going around the place barefoot. Still, my feet deserved to be free even though I couldn't be.

Caiman held me steady as I swayed. This music was terrible. Were the musicians playing from different songs? "You can barely stand. What were you thinking, drinking that much?" he said through his teeth, his smile brittle as he nodded to men in black dinner jackets and women in fancy hats.

"I was thinking I needed to be drunk to marry you."

The muscles in his jaw worked. I could hear his teeth grinding together. The musicians stopped their terrible whinging to strike up a slow waltz. Caiman took my hand in his, slipping it onto his shoulder. The definition beneath his jacket came as a shock. When we were younger, he'd been so skinny. He was still slim, nothing like his broad-shouldered brother, but there was strength there too. I clasped his gloved hand, the leather warm and soft. His free hand found my waist, pulling me toward him. The space between us, although conventional, felt too small.

He was too close.

Too warm.

Too overwhelming.

All that wine may have been a bad idea.

When he began the steps, my own feet were slow to move. We'd only taken three turns when the room began spinning. "Oh no . . ." My face felt hot and sweaty, and even though Caiman stopped, the people watching us were still going around and around and around, a swirl of color and motion, and if they didn't stop, I was going to get—

Caiman's arm slipped around my waist, towing me

toward a room concealed in the paneling behind the dais, a trail of catcalls and jolly laughter following.

Caiman wasn't laughing, though. Did he even know how? He looked like he wanted to murder someone. Broderick appeared out of nowhere to open the door. Beads of perspiration collected on my brow. My stomach heaved, and I vomited all over the tiles.

Caiman cursed, catching me before I collapsed.

"I think I'm dying," I groaned, my throat burning and tongue tasting like bile.

"You're not dying. You're drunk." Strong arms collected me against a solid chest. Doors opened and closed. Squeezing my eyes shut, I prayed the queasiness would subside. When I felt steady enough to open them again, I really did think I would die.

"Where are we?" This wasn't my room. My room was light and airy, gold and blue.

This room had been decorated with mahogany and emerald green, from the vines on the patterned wallpaper, to the four poster bed, to the heavy drapes on either side of a double-height window.

Caiman set me on the foot of the bed and went to speak to someone at the door. *Broderick.* They exchanged words in low tones, glancing at me every so often. I couldn't stay in here. Alone. With *him.* There had to be an exit somewhere. There were two doors in addition to the one Caiman blocked, but there was no telling where they would lead. Knowing him, it could be some sort of torture chamber.

A moment later, the door clicked closed, and I found myself utterly alone with my husband.

11

CAIMAN

THE DOOR CLOSED, AND I RESISTED THE OVERWHELMING urge to call Broderick back. Why had I brought Roisin here instead of her mother's chambers? She may have been expected to spend the night with me—someone would be in to check the sheets in the morning—but she was drunk as a bloomin' lark. Surely the council would understand my refusal to sleep with her when she could barely stand.

Besides, this wasn't what either of us wanted.

I glanced at my new wife from over my shoulder, finding her turned away toward the adjoining study, clutching the wall.

It isn't what one *of us wanted,* I silently amended.

The moment she'd entered the chapel, the air had escaped my lungs, and I hadn't been able to catch my breath since. She should've been marrying Alrec, but by some twisted turn of fate, she had married me. She'd promised to love and honor me without the slightest tremor in her voice.

Me. No one else.

She didn't have a choice, I knew that.

And yet I allowed myself to pretend for those few

90

precious moments that this was real. That I loved her, and she loved me, and that we were going to rule this kingdom together, a true partnership in every way. My worries and fears faded until all that remained were the two of us speaking words we didn't mean.

I hadn't been able to keep my eyes off of her at dinner. Every time her hair fell over her collarbone, my fingers itched to brush it away. None of her smiles had been for me, but it hadn't mattered because she had been smiling.

"Is this your room?" Roisin choked, bringing me back to the present. She stumbled for the bed, falling onto the edge of the mattress.

"It is." My room. My bed. My wife.

Should I go to her?

I should go to her.

I took a few steps forward but stopped when I saw her stiffen. "Would you like some water?" I asked, my mouth dry as soot.

She looked so small and meek, clasping her hands in her lap before nodding.

I went to the jug on the desk and poured two glasses. When I offered her one, she hesitated before taking it. I drank until my glass was empty before replacing it on the desk. "Feeling any better?"

Her eyes flicked to mine, glowing ever so slightly like silver stars. Did they always do that in the dark, or was it the drink? "Worse."

She must've had at least a bottle and a half on her own. How she drank that rot was beyond me. I could barely stomach our own liquor, let alone the shite the faeries brewed.

"Thank you for the water. I'm ready to return to my

own chambers," she announced, setting the glass on the bedside table and smoothing a hand down her ivory skirts.

"Your chambers have been given to Lord and Lady Stanton." My cousins had made the four-day journey from Bishopstown for Alrec's wedding. Instead, they had attended his funeral and watched me steal his bride.

His kingdom.

His life.

Roisin's eyes bulged, and I swore I could taste her panic as she clutched my quilt. "Where are my things?"

"Being moved."

"Moved where?"

"Some of your dresses are in there." I pointed to the second armoire that had been added only yesterday. "And the rest will be stored until our new rooms are prepared." When my father was gone, we would occupy the king and queen's suites. Until then, we would stay here.

"*Our* rooms . . ." She shot to her feet, catching herself on one of the mahogany bedposts. "I cannot share a bedroom with you."

The clenching in my stomach turned to a deep, sharp ache. "You will have your own chambers if that is how you wish to live." I would never force her to do anything she wasn't comfortable with. Although I hoped eventually she'd stay with me. My mother and father had shared a room until the day she passed. We were far from a love match like they had been, but in time, hopefully we would find our way. The kingdom would need heirs, after all.

My heart sped at the thought.

She started shaking her head, wide eyes searching the darkness. "I want my own chambers now."

Hadn't her mother explained to her what would happen after we wed? At eighteen, she should know what transpired between a husband and wife. With my face burning, I cleared my throat and said, "It is expected . . ." No, that wasn't the right word. "What I meant to say was, it is customary for a husband and wife to stay together on their wedding night."

The choked noise she made sounded like a dying cat. "We may technically be married, but I am no more your wife than you are my husband. Everything I promised you today was a lie," she slurred, narrowing bloodshot eyes at me. "I hate you."

"That may be so, but we are married. And with that comes certain responsibilities."

She backed toward the wall, knocking the locker on her way past. The glass fell to the ground, spilling water across the carpet. "If you touch me, I will scream."

Even in my worst temper, I had never been violent toward her—or any woman. When she and her friends threw food at me, called me names, I took it. When they attacked my character in front of an audience, slandered me to my peers, I bit my tongue. "What have I done to make you think I would force you to do something you don't want to do?"

"I know about you and Lady Whitney."

Memories crashed into me like a fist to the jaw. Dark hair. Violet eyes. A warm smile and honey-sweet voice. "Who told you about Lady Whitney?" There were only four people in this world who knew about what had happened to her. Only three of them knew the truth. And one of them was dead.

"Your brother," she sneered, her hands balling into fists. "The only man I'll ever love. The one I should've married."

Did she really think it necessary to remind me at every turn that I wasn't supposed to be here? That this shouldn't have been my wedding night? That the throne belonged to someone else? That *she* belonged to someone else?

"And what did your *beloved* Alrec tell you about Lady Whitney?" It obviously wasn't the truth. Because if it was, she never would've fallen in love with him.

"That he had to save the poor woman from your unwanted advances—had to pull you off of her. And when you resisted, he broke your jaw."

Did her foolish love for my brother really make her that blind?

I stalked forward, ready to unload the truth about what had happened that day. Until Roisin flinched. I shrank back. The woman appeared genuinely terrified.

"At least now I understand why you hate me." What other lies had he whispered these past four years? Could that be why she'd chosen him over me? Why hadn't I fought harder to win her affections? Why had I given in so easily?

He's the heir.

I'd given in because I'd had nothing—been nothing.

Breathing through my frustration, I withdrew the decorative sword at my hip. "My brother was not good. Nor was he kind." I waited for her to ask me why. To beg for clarity. To seek the truth and dismiss the lies.

Instead, she stared at me through glowing silver eyes, silent as the night around us.

I ripped the glove from my left hand and drew the blade across my palm. The slicing pain did nothing but stir my ire as I threw the bedcovers aside and clenched my fist, letting blood dribble over the white sheets. "The man you claim to love was a fallacy. He lied to you about what happened with Lady Whitney, and I can say with complete confidence that if he'd had the honor of becoming your husband, if he was the one standing here tonight, he wouldn't take 'no' for an answer."

I shoved my sword back into its scabbard and turned toward the door, not knowing where I would go, only that I had to get away from her. We may have been expected to spend tonight together, but I refused to put her in a position where she felt unsafe. Even if that meant we never shared a bed. Eventually, she had to realize I wasn't the villain in this story.

My hand stilled on the doorknob.

Except . . . I was the villain.

I was the reason my brother was dead.

I opened the door and slipped into the hallway, sounds from the ballroom echoing from the far end, toward the staircase.

Broderick startled when he saw me.

"Stay here," I told him. "Make sure no one bothers the princess."

He nodded, albeit reluctantly. "Where will you go?"

"Does it matter?" I scrubbed a hand down my face, weariness making my bones feel like lead. I retreated toward the solace of the library.

A familiar voice drawled my name. Lord Kerrington sauntered toward me from the staircase, Lowri on his arm.

"Finished already?" Kerrington clicked his tongue.

I wouldn't hit him because that would be wrong. A king didn't punch his subjects for being rude. A king ignored them or had someone punch them for him.

"Poor Roisin," he chuckled, shaking his head. "Didn't even get a good ride on her wedding night. If you need me to step in, I could—"

My fist slammed into his nose, and it felt like I'd

punched a damned brick wall. Blood poured down his lips, his chin, all over his blue waistcoat.

"You broke my damned nose!" he howled, letting go of Lowri's arm to cradle his swelling face.

"Alrec isn't here to hide behind anymore," I reminded him, biting back the urge to groan at my aching hand. I'd definitely broken something. *Dammit.* How had Alrec throttled me so many times and not shed one tear? "And if you ever speak of my wife like that again, I will have your head on a pike. Do I make myself clear?"

Kerrington's eyes blazed before he bowed his head, blood leaking from his face onto the floor. "Perfectly, *your highness.*" With that, he turned on his heel and stomped toward the exit.

Lowri swayed. I caught her before she fell face-first into the wall. She smelled as if she'd bathed in drink. "Where are your friends, Lady Lowri?"

"I only have . . . two friends. One, you just . . . punched, and the other . . . you *married* her. How . . . how *could* you?" Two hiccups later, she was sobbing into my arms. What was it with this woman and crying?

"Come. I'll bring you back to the ball." Once I handed her off to a responsible party, I'd find a place to sleep.

"W-why are you being nice to me?"

"Because I am too exhausted to be anything else."

She swiped at her wet cheeks, frowning toward the ballroom. "I don't want to go back in. People look at me as if I don't belong here."

"They do not."

"Yes, they do," she insisted, sniffling as more tears welled in her turquoise eyes. "They see my ears and my hair and my eyes and *whisper.* I hate it. I wish I could be like one of you."

I understood wanting to be someone else. Not that I'd wanted to be like Alrec. I'd just wanted to be the person people looked to instead of looked past.

I had gotten my wish, and now all I wanted was to hide.

"Why would you want to be one of us when you get to be you?"

The look she gave me, all furrowed brow and searching eyes, left me slowing my pace as we approached the small room she'd been assigned, just off the queen's suite.

"You can come in if you'd like," she whispered, her cheeks turning pink.

There was no chance I was going into a bedchamber with another woman. Still, I didn't want to sound like an ass, so I lied and said, "I want to return to my wife."

A wife who didn't want me.

A wife who hated me.

A wife who believed I was a violent reprobate.

Lowri nodded and slipped into her room. The moment the door clicked into place, I went to find somewhere to sleep.

12

____

ROISIN

IF THE CLOCK ON THE DESK DIDN'T STOP TICKING SO LOUDLY, I was going to throw it out the window. I'd come to the library for a bit of peace and quiet, but the room's double-height ceiling made every sound echo, and the smell of musty pages left my stomach churning like a stormy sea.

"And then he punched Lord Kerrington square in the nose!" Lowri poured me another glass of water from the jug beside the clock. The giggling. The swooshing of her wide green skirts. The *click-click* of her shoes on the wooden planks. All of it made me want to rip out my hair.

"Must you be so loud?" I breathed, pinching the bridge of my nose and screwing my eyes shut against the sunlight bursting through the open windows. If I'd had the energy, I would've pulled the heavy drapes. But then there wouldn't be a breeze, and the smells in this room would put me in an early grave. "Why is it so hot in this blasted castle?" I fanned myself with my hand, wishing my things hadn't been packed away so I could've brought an actual fan.

The color of my dress reminded me of pea soup. It was

like whoever had supervised the relocation of my garments had stuffed the ugliest ones into Caiman's armoire.

Caiman.

The thought of where I'd stayed last night left me shuddering.

At least now I know why you hate me.

How could I do anything but hate him, knowing the awful things he'd said? The unforgivable things he'd done?

He lied to you about what happened . . .

That was the part I couldn't wrap my muddled head around. Caiman had appeared genuinely shocked when I'd brought up Lady Whitney's name. It could've been guilt that had flickered across his expression. But the frustration and hurt in his tone left me wondering. What if all the other awful stories Alrec had told me were wrong as well? No. He'd loved me—had wanted to keep me from getting hurt. He wouldn't have lied to me for all these years. Not about his own brother.

I wrapped my fingers around the cool glass and took a drink, letting the lukewarm liquid soothe my dry throat.

Lowri giggled again. "You should have seen the prince. He was brilliant—like a dark, avenging angel, swooping in and"—she balled her hand into a fist and punched the air—"*Pow.* There was blood everywhere."

"Why did he strike him?" Had Caiman taken his pent-up frustration with me out on someone else?

"Haven't you been listening?" The cushion dipped when Lowri threw herself beside me. "Kerrington made some snide remark about husbandly duties, and Caiman lost his mind."

"It's Caiman, now, is it?" For some reason, hearing her use his given name made my stomach clench. Or it could've been the water mixing with whatever was left after I'd vomited all over *Caiman's* boots.

"I'm convinced he's not as awful as we originally thought." Her head fell back, sending her violet hair cascading over the sofa's rich leather arm. "He even walked me to my chambers."

Caiman hadn't returned to his room, and I hadn't seen him this morning when the servants brought breakfast to the solar. Had he stayed with her? Surely not. My friend wouldn't have slept with my husband on my wedding night.

Was that a smile? It was. Lowri was smiling. Why was she smiling? Was it a secret smile? A sleepy one? Was she thinking about him? "Did he . . . Did he accompany you inside?"

She fiddled with the ribbon around her waist, letting the lace slip through her fingers as she stared longingly toward the ceiling. "I offered, but he declined."

"What do you mean, you 'offered'?" I choked.

"Only as a test," she said with a dismissive wave. "To see if he was the wretch we always believed him to be. He's not, by the way. If he wasn't so damned serious all the time, I dare say he could be sweet."

What would I have done if he'd accepted? What would *she* have done? Before I could ask, the man in question strolled into the library. My face flushed, and Lowri's smile grew as her eyes raked from Caiman's dark waistcoat to his black boots. When he noticed us, he twisted away as if to escape, ramming straight into Broderick's broad frame blocking the exit.

Caiman turned back around with a grimace and bobbed his head. "Good morning."

Lowri jumped to her feet, dipping into a low curtsy. "Good morning, your highness. I trust you slept well."

"Quite. And you?"

"Very well, thank you."

What were they? The best of friends? "Lowri? Could you be a dear and run down the hall to grab my shawl? It's rather drafty today."

"Are you mad?" She wiped her brow with the back of her hand. "It's like an oven in here."

Broderick nudged Caiman.

Caiman gave him a confused look. Broderick rolled his eyes and nodded toward me.

"I . . . ah . . . I have a coat. You can have it if you'd like." Before Caiman could slip his arms free, I stopped him with a raised hand.

"That is too kind. But I would prefer my own shawl. Lowri?"

Although her eyes narrowed, she bobbed a curtsy and spun toward the exit. Broderick glanced between Caiman and I before following her out the door.

Shifting his weight from one foot to the other, Caiman shoved his hands deep into his pockets as he looked everywhere in the room but at me. "Are you feeling better?"

If anything, my headache had worsened. I'd only managed a few bites of toast at breakfast. Hopefully, lunch would be more appealing. "No. But it's a discomfort of my own making, so I must suffer through." It was too bad my healing magic didn't work on hangovers.

Awkward silence fell, punctuated by the ticking clock.

"Right. Well, I'd best be off." He started for the back of the library, toward dark tapestries and dusty tomes on towering shelves.

"Would you like to sit with me?" I blurted before my brain could catch up with my mouth.

Caiman ran straight into one of the bookshelves, cursing

and holding it steady so it didn't topple over. I set the empty glass aside and patted the cushion, still dented from Lowri.

I found myself holding my breath as he closed the gap between us and sank onto the sofa. I breathed in his subtle, spicy scent, feeling traitorous for liking it so much. Instead of looking at me, he stared toward the vacant fireplace. Above the mantle hung a beautiful painting of a ship sailing a violent sea, turquoise waves crashing across the deck.

"That's a nice painting," I said.

Caiman stared at the thing as though he'd never seen it before. "I hate it."

Of course he did. Caiman hated everything. Instead of telling him as much, I asked why he hated it.

"It's depressing, isn't it?"

"I think it's dramatic." The ship's torn sails and the way it seemed to be careening straight for the shore left me waiting for the sound of a hull crashing on the jagged rocks jutting from the water. "Good art should evoke emotion."

His head tilted as he considered. "Eh . . . I still hate it. There are far nicer pieces in the back." He stood and started toward the tapestries. "Are you coming or not?"

My stomach lurched when I stood, but I recovered quickly, following him past shelves and shelves of so many books it would take ten lifetimes to finish them all. The air grew mustier the farther we went, and the brightness faded. He told me to wait and disappeared behind one of the last shelves. There was a clatter and a curse, and then Caiman emerged and gestured toward the murky darkness to where an oil painting of a field teaming with bright wildflowers and distant snow-capped mountains leaned against the far wall. But it wasn't the scenery that stole my breath.

In the center of the flowers, with her hair in a long braid

over her shoulder, sat a pink-haired faerie with luminescent wings.

My heart began to pound in my chest. "Why do you like this one?"

His response was barely more than a whisper as he stared reverently at the painting. "When I found out one of us was to marry a fae, I went searching for anything and everything I could find on your people. There were very few books left from when the fae occupied this island, most of the records having been destroyed along with the histories of magic. I found this in a dusty old attic." The barest hint of a smile crossed his lips. "This was how I imagined you. The wings. The ears. The hair. All of it."

I hadn't thought of what it would've been like for him to meet us for the first time. He must've been as nervous as me —perhaps more so since we had magic on our side.

"Were you disappointed when you realized I didn't have wings?" Although faeries and fae weren't the same, people often confused the two. There were still clans of winged faeries around Iodale and Airren, but they were becoming more rare with each passing decade.

His startled chuckle warmed me to my toes. "No, Roisin. I was not disappointed." Sighing, he started back toward the main entrance. When we reached the sofa, he paused, as if trying to decide if he should stay or go. It surprised me how much I wanted him to stay.

"I need to apologize for last night." I still couldn't believe I'd had the gall to speak to him so terribly. "I was horrible and I'm sorry."

"You have been horrible to me for years." Wincing, he flexed his gloved hands. "Why are you bothering to apologize now?"

Flickers of embarrassment burned my cheeks. I may

have been horrible to him, but he had been horrible to me as well, and he had never once apologized. "Never mind. I take it back. I'm not sorry anymore."

He caught my wrist before I could run for the door. "Don't go. Please. I didn't mean it like that." He let me go just as quickly, scrubbing a gloved hand down his black breeches, a faint blush creeping along his jaw. "I just . . . I don't understand what differentiates the way you treated me last night from the way you've been treating me for the past four years."

Leaving wouldn't solve anything. So I sank onto the sofa and spread my hideous green skirt to hide the fact that I hadn't bothered with shoes. "You are my husband now." Whether we liked it or not, we were stuck together. "I am trying. All I ask is that you do the same."

I expected him to tell me off. To call me names and tell me what I could do with my apology.

He simply nodded and said, "All right."

Something akin to hope swelled in my broken heart. "That's it? All right?"

He tugged on the ends of his gloves, sinking onto the cushion next to me. "I would like to try as well."

When he stretched his hand again and winced, I remembered Lowri's story and the way he'd cut his palm before he left me. If the pain tightening his mouth was any indication, it must be frightfully sore. "Show me your hand."

He shoved both hands behind his back like a child caught with stolen sweets. "No." His brow furrowed. "Why?"

"I heard you got into a fight."

His gaze flicked to mine, dark eyes searching. "He deserved it."

"I have no doubt." Although I considered Lord Kerrington a friend, he was not without his faults. I held my hand toward Caiman. "Let me fix it. It's the least I can do."

The way his nose wrinkled and eyes narrowed—he looked genuinely horrified. "I don't want you to fix it."

She is a monster.

An abomination.

"Does my magic disgust you so much that you'd rather be in pain than let me touch you?"

A wrinkle formed between his eyebrows. "Why on earth would you think that?"

"It doesn't matter." This was a lost cause. We were a lost cause.

"*Dammit.*" He ripped off his glove and held his bandaged hand toward me. "Here."

I'd been prepared for the bandages, blood, and bruised knuckles. What I hadn't expected were the vicious scars dimpling the back of his hand, stretching across his forearms, and disappearing beneath his shirtsleeve.

My heart sank as I took his hand in mine, tracing the deep pits and grooves and gnarled bumps of poorly healed skin. "What happened?" These scars hadn't been there when I had grabbed his hands and walked with him through the gardens years ago.

"I almost beat Alrec in a race . . . until he . . . he pushed me into a bonfire."

My breath caught. The Alrec I knew never would've hurt someone like that.

The man you loved was a fallacy.

What if it was true and I'd been a fool all this time? What if everything I knew had been a lie?

If I'd truly misjudged Alrec so terribly, had I misjudged Caiman as well?

Except I'd *heard* Caiman speaking with Alrec that day, saying terrible things about me.

How could I trust myself knowing someone I loved may have been fooling me all these years? How did I know Caiman wasn't taking advantage of me too?

She is a monster.

I shook my head against the memory. We'd been young. I may have been enamored with Caiman, but that didn't mean he had felt the same about me. And it didn't change the fact that we were married now and needed to find a way to heal the wounds of our past and move forward together.

I untied the bandages wrapped around Caiman's palm to find the edges of the self-inflicted wound angry and red. Closing my eyes, I called upon my power, searching for its familiar heat and sending it toward him, feeling it travel from my body to his.

The wounds were small, and yet the pain in him was as great as that of the man I'd felt dying in the courtyard. Beads of sweat collected on my brow, and the room began to spin. It felt as if I was falling into a pit with no light and no end, swallowing me, dragging me under.

"Roisin?" The concern in Caiman's soft tone brought me back from the darkness.

I opened my eyes to find him staring, brow furrowed and lips turned down. Although the wound across his palm had healed and his knuckles no longer showed damage, the scars remained.

"There. All better," I whispered, licking my dry lips. For a split second, I could've sworn his gaze dropped to my mouth. I offered my husband a tentative smile, clutching the edge of the cushion to keep from passing out. My limbs felt as if I had swum across the sea.

"Thank you." Caiman lifted a scarred hand to brush

aside a strand of hair that had fallen over my shoulder. Every nerve in my body sparked to life as his fingers lingered, tracing my bare collarbone.

"You could never disgust me," he said as if it were some deep, dark confession.

All this time, I'd thought his eyes were black, but they weren't. They were the darkest shade of brown, like a cup of the strongest tea.

And his lips . . .

If I leaned toward him, ours would meet. Perhaps this was the way we started over. The way we moved forward.

"Your shawl, milady," Lowri clipped from the doorway.

Caiman clattered to his feet as if we'd been caught doing something far more scandalous than sharing a sofa. I pressed my spine into the cushions at my back, desperate to calm my uneven breathing before anyone noticed. If only the ferocious blush creeping up my neck were as easy to control. "Thank you, Lowri." I took the offered garment, wrapping it around my overwarm shoulders.

I could've sworn a smile ghosted across Broderick's face from his post at the door.

"You should refer to her as 'your highness,'" Caiman said. Although he had spoken to Lowri, his gaze remained fixed on me. "She is, after all, my wife."

"My apologies, *your highness*," Lowri amended with a curtsy.

Caiman nodded and left the room. Perhaps being married to a dark prince wouldn't be so bad after all.

Lowri propped her fists on her hips. "So?"

"So, what?"

"So yesterday you were all 'I hate him' and last night you refused to let him in your bed. And then today you're all 'let me stare into your eyes until I drown.'"

I immediately regretted telling Lowri what had happened after the marriage feast. It was none of her business anyway. "Why is your opinion the only one allowed to change?"

"Because I'm not the one in love with his brother."

Guilt tugged at my core. Was I to hate Caiman for eternity because I had loved Alrec? Should I wear my grief like a shroud for everyone to see so they didn't judge me too harshly for trying to move on? "I am trying to make the best of things, Lowri."

But to do that, I would need to know if I could truly trust Caiman.

I needed to learn the truth.

My legs shook as I made my way to a heavily carved mahogany writing desk beneath a painting of what I assumed was one of Caiman's ancestors.

Lowri watched with a furrowed brow as I searched the drawers for a fountain pen. Once I found one, I pulled a small card from a stack and wrote a note to Lady Whitney.

13

CAIMAN

TODAY HAD BEEN ONE OF THE BEST DAYS OF MY LIFE. WHICH was pathetic, really, since nothing had actually happened. It could've, though. If only Lowri hadn't interrupted when she did. I traced a finger down my new silver scar, different from all the others on my hands.

Who was I kidding? It wasn't Lowri's fault. It was mine.

I was a coward.

Roisin had been so close, magic sparkling in her quicksilver eyes. *So bloomin' close.* All I had to do was lean forward. Instead, I started wondering if I was misreading the situation. What if she hadn't wanted me to kiss her? She could've closed the gap herself, and yet she hadn't.

My father tossed and turned, the sheets twisting around his torso as he cried out in his dreams. No moonlight fell through the window, only darkness. My eyes had long since adjusted to the lack of light. I'd abandoned my coat and waistcoat ages ago, yet sweat still collected beneath my arms. My father's teeth chattered despite the mound of fur blankets piled on top of him.

Today may have been the best day, but tonight felt like

one of the worst nights. The sour smell of sickness clung to the heavy air. The royal physician had left an hour ago. On his way out, he had claimed the end was near. As much as I longed for the solace of sleep, I wanted to be with my father when he passed. No one should have to die alone.

Alrec had died alone, mortally wounded by cannon fire, tossed into the sea by a sinking ship. At least that's what the eye-witness reports had said. I hoped he didn't suffer. That he'd been gone before the waves had swallowed his body.

My mother had died alone as well.

Someone knocked softly at the door, and a woman popped her head inside. My heart beat double-time when I saw silver hair.

"You called for me, your highness?"

Not Roisin but her mother.

I stood and smoothed a hand down my breeches, trying to make it look like I was keeping it together instead of falling apart. "Come in. Please."

She swept in as quiet as a breeze, glancing sidelong at my father when he whimpered. What must it be like for the fae, to not have to worry about something as final as death?

"The physician says there isn't much time left," I explained, fighting a losing battle with my tears.

Lady Seren's mouth flattened, her expression grim.

"Would you be willing to check him? I know there isn't much to be done, but if there is any way to ease his suffering, I would forever be in your debt."

"Say no more." She went to my father's bed, drawing down the layers of quilts to reveal the white tunic swallowing his withered frame. After unlacing the front, she pressed her hands to his heart. When her eyes fell closed, I closed mine as well, praying to whoever would listen. If he was to go, let it be quickly and without pain. But if there was any way for him to stay . . . I knew how selfish it sounded, but I prayed for that most of all.

"Caiman?"

When I opened my eyes, I found my father sitting up, his back propped against the headboard. Was I dreaming? I must be. He hadn't been lucid since the wedding.

"Thank you, Lady Seren." My father patted her hand and gave her a wry smile.

She kissed his forehead, firelight glistening off the tears streaming down her cheeks. "My king."

I rushed to his side and dropped onto the bed, taking his weathered hand in mine. "Father . . . you look . . ."

"Like a bloomin' corpse," he chuckled. When he squeezed my fingers, his grip felt as strong as ever.

He didn't look like a corpse. The color had returned to his cheeks; the spark had returned to his eyes. "You look well."

"What'd I teach you about lying, son?"

"You look better," I amended. That last bit of magic had brought him back to me. How could Roisin think I found her magic disgusting? I had watched her heal broken men, had seen her mother heal my father. And she'd healed me as well, of my twisted leg and breathing troubles that had plagued me since birth.

Magic was a gift.

When he drew in a deep breath, his chest no longer rattled, and my hope grew along with my smile.

"Do you care to tell me why you're sitting in here with an old man instead of with your new wife?"

My smile faltered. The last thing I wanted was to disappoint him and set him back in his healing. "It's complicated." That sounded good enough, right? It was certainly the truth. And I couldn't explain how complicated it was without upsetting him. He'd already lost too much.

His blue eyes lifted heavenward. "Two people from different backgrounds trying to make a life together is complicated? You don't say."

"Your sarcasm is not appreciated."

He gave my hand another squeeze. His grip felt even stronger. "Son, I've been married four times to four different women. It's always complicated."

But it was more than that. The other women my father had married must've held him in some regard at the very least. And I knew for a fact that my mother had loved the man. The same could not be said for my wife. I'd been cast as the villain in her story since I was fifteen. It would take a great deal of time and effort to change her opinion of me— if it was even possible. "Roisin does not care for me." What I'd felt today in the library must've been a fluke, my own latent desire playing tricks.

"That is because she does not know you." The mattress shifted as he eased forward to lay a steady hand on my shoulder. "And she will not learn to know you if you insist on hiding in my chambers."

Hiding away was far easier than facing what awaited me in my own room. A man could only take so much rejection.

The new silver scar on my hand felt smooth beneath my fingertip. "And if she doesn't care for what she learns?" If she found out that I was responsible for Alrec's death? What then? She would never forgive me for taking away the man she loved.

My father patted my cheek with a dry hand the way he used to when I was a boy. "Marriage is like connecting two islands in the vast sea. As long as you're both building a bridge in the right direction, you will find each other eventually."

Today was our first step in the right direction. I'd shown her one of my most guarded secrets—my hands. She hadn't laughed or made fun of the way my twisted, mangled scars made it look as if I wore my veins outside my skin.

My brother and I had both had far too much to drink that night two years ago. He'd been taunting me over winning Roisin's affections, had shown me one of the letters she'd written him. In front of a crowd of people, he told me that if I could beat him in a race, I could have her. Simple as that.

He had cared so little that he'd bet his betrothal on a bloomin' footrace.

My hatred for him had been enough to fuel me. And my love for her had given me the advantage.

And I would've won if he hadn't shoved me into a bloody bonfire.

My father chuckled. "Go to her. And have faith in yourself. I certainly do."

I wanted to, but how could I leave him? I'd have a lifetime with Roisin. There was no telling how much longer my father would be with me. And after what had happened with Mother . . . "Morning is soon enough."

Rolling his eyes, he gave my shoulder a shove. "If you're staying for me, don't. I won't get a moment of rest knowing my son is in here staring at me, listening to me snore."

I tried to read his eyes, no longer jaundiced but clear. "Are you certain you're feeling all right?"

"Son, I've never felt better."

I gave him a fierce hug before racing toward the privy chamber, where Broderick stood next to the window. Hadn't

I told him to make himself comfortable? Did the man ever sit down?

When he saw me, he turned fully and offered a bow. "How is the king?"

"Much better thanks to Lady Seren." I continued past him, toward the outer door. "Come. I need your help." It was time to get to know my wife.

Although I hadn't been in the castle's kitchens in years, I found my way without issue. Once I reached the basement rooms, my bravado waned. Where the hell did they keep all the food? There were copper pots aplenty, dangling from hooks on the stone walls. Fireplaces and stoves, tables and chairs, and enough wooden spoons to supply an entire army, but unless I wanted to feed my bride raw onions and potatoes, the trip had been pointless.

Broderick proved almost as useless when it came to scavenging for sustenance. We managed to find some scones wrapped in a tea towel along with a few sticks of dried beef, two apples more bruised than not, and a bottle of faerie wine to pack into an oversized basket Broderick insisted on carrying. By the time we reached my bedchamber, I was so full of nerves and excitement, I didn't think I'd sleep for a week.

It felt strange knocking on my own door, but barging in would set the wrong tone. A moment later, Roisin answered, her glorious hair tumbling loose about her silk-clad shoulders. When she saw me, she squinted as if she wasn't sure I was really there. "Have you lost your mind, Caiman? It's the middle of the night."

I loved the way she said my name. *There. I admitted it.* She could be shouting at me or giving out, and I'd take it all as long as she was saying my name instead of calling me one of the terrible nicknames she and her friends had given me over the years.

"I know. But I wanted to see you." When I turned to retrieve the basket from my guard, I found him red-faced, staring at the wall. "And I brought a picnic."

She looked at me as if I'd lost my mind. Maybe I had. "Is there anything good?"

"Scones and wine."

I couldn't believe it when she opened the door wider and told me to come inside.

Roisin had only been staying in my room for two nights, and yet it already smelled like her. I tried not to look toward the unmade bed where she'd been sleeping, warm and snuggled—and presumably without the silk robe tied hastily around her slender waist.

My stomach tightened as I turned toward the fireplace and set the basket on the rug. After being in my father's suffocating room, the space felt chilly. I added a few coals to the grate and banked the fire while she unpacked the picnic.

"Did you bring plates?" she asked, elbow-deep in the basket. The crackling fire made her silver waves glisten like icicles.

Bollocks. "No."

A smile played on her lips as she withdrew the cork from the wine and shook the bottle. "How about glasses?"

I shook my head.

"This is the worst picnic I've ever been on," she said with a laugh, taking a sip directly from the bottle.

"Then go back to bed and I will eat and drink on my

own." I snagged the bottle from her and took a swig, my stomach instantly revolting at the taste of sour fruit.

She stole it back and grinned before taking another sip. "You woke me, which means you have to feed me."

"Is that some fae law I don't know about?"

"If it's not, it should be." She handed me a scone before peering back into the empty basket. "There's no butter either, is there?"

Dammit. "Next time, you can organize the picnic."

"Agreed."

Meaning there would be a next time. I'd feed her midnight picnics for as long as she'd let me.

"What brings you to my room at"—she glanced toward the clock—"half two in the morning?"

The bottle in my hand shook when I brought it to my lips. "Technically, it's *my* room."

Her cheeks flushed, and I made the mistake of looking toward the bed. Her gaze followed mine, and her blush spread to her neck, down her throat, to her chest.

"Don't worry, I'm not here to perform my husbandly duties." Unless she wanted to. Then I would absolutely rise to the occasion.

Her gaze dropped to the half-eaten scone in her hand.

Right. No duties tonight. But she didn't tell me there was no way in hell it would ever happen, so I took her lack of response as a small victory. "I am here to build a bridge," I said, handing off the bottle in favor of a bruised apple that tasted almost as bad as the wine. I only managed two sour bites before throwing it into the fire.

Roisin's brow furrowed as she picked a raisin from the scone and popped it into her mouth. "What does that mean?"

"I was speaking with my father tonight, and he said—"

She reached for my knee. "You spoke with him tonight?"

She was touching me. Willingly. *Dammit.* I needed to calm down and focus on something besides how amazing the heat from her hand felt burning through my breeches. I looked at the bed again. And now I was looking at her mouth.

Where was that wine? I gripped the bottle's slender neck and took another gulp. "I did. Just before I came here."

Her fingers contracted. "How is he?"

"He?" I choked, fire burning in my belly.

"Your father."

Yes. My father. Bloomin' hell, I was on the verge of madness. "He's doing much better, thank you."

"I am happy to hear that. He is a good man."

Not only was he good, he was wise as well. When she went to remove her hand, I caught her fingers. Instead of pulling away, she scooted closer, spilling crumbs from her lap all over the rug.

"May I ask you something?" she whispered, her eyes fixed on our joined hands.

"Of course."

She turned my hand over to trace the skin at the underside of my wrist. Her lips lifted in a slight smile. Her full, pouty lips. "Where have you been sleeping?"

"On a dreadfully uncomfortable chair in my father's chambers."

Her gaze darted to mine before returning to my wrist. "Oh . . ."

Bare feet peeked from beneath her shift as she inched closer, her bent knees now firmly against my outstretched leg. She'd always had dainty feet.

"Why do you ask?"

"It's silly." She set my hand in her lap to collect the wine and down three quick swallows, grimacing when she set it aside. Then she took my hand to resume her exploration, tugging the hem of my glove a little higher, exposing the wound she'd healed. My palms weren't as mangled as the backs of my hands, but the thick scar tissue had left me with little sensation. Somehow, I could feel every swipe of her nail as she traced not only the scar but the lines in my palm as well.

I didn't care how silly it was, I wanted to know. Desperately. "Tell me anyway."

Her shoulders rose and fell with her exaggerated sigh. "When you didn't come back, I thought perhaps you found somewhere else to stay."

"I did. With my father." I'd already said that, hadn't I?

Her hair spilled across her chest when she shook her head. The tie at her waist had come loose, leaving the front of her robe hanging open. Lace covered the top of her shift. I longed to trace the deep V at the front the way she traced my palm.

"I cannot believe you're forcing me to say this aloud," she muttered, her finger stilling. "I assumed you'd been sleeping with someone else, you fool."

"On our wedding night?" I choked.

She buried her face in her hands, muffling her groan. "I told you it was silly, didn't I?"

It wasn't silly. It was sad. She truly thought the worst of me.

I drew her hands away, waiting for her eyes to lock with mine. "Allow me to make something perfectly clear: When we exchanged vows, I meant every promise I made. To honor and cherish you. And to remain faithful. I hope that in time you will see it for yourself."

Her eyes glistened with unshed tears as she pulled free of my grasp. "I want to see the goodness in you, but all I see is a man who thinks I am a monster."

"I don't think you're a monster."

"Maybe not anymore, but you did."

"I never—"

"Deny it all you want, but I heard you with my own ears. You told Alrec I was nothing more than a hideous monster trying to weasel her way to a throne."

My heart stuttered to a stop.

Dammit. How in the hell had she heard me? My brother and I had been alone. I'd made sure of it. That night I'd said such vicious, slanderous things. Had she heard them all?

"If my brother thought for a second that I wanted you, he would have stopped at nothing to take you from me." It didn't matter what it was. Toys, treats, friends—if I had it, Alrec wanted it to be his and his alone. "I would've done anything to have you as my bride, including calling you terrible names that couldn't be further from the truth." I'd hoped that he wouldn't pursue her, leaving her to me. In the end, it didn't matter. She'd chosen him, sealing both our fates.

"How was I to know?"

"All you had to do was ask me why I said the things I did. I would've explained everything. Instead, you took one conversation out of context and have made me pay for it ever since."

She flinched at my words, tears welling in her eyes. "It doesn't matter now."

"No. It doesn't." I stood, ice replacing the heat in my veins as I stalked toward the exit, desperate for silence so I could collect my thoughts without *her* staring at me. The rickety bridge I'd tried to build turned to rubble. Roisin would never trust me. Considering the other secret I kept, how could I blame her? I was every bit the villain she believed me to be. She would be far better off without someone like me in her life.

When I yanked open the door, Broderick had his hand raised as if to knock. Behind him, Lord Devon waited next to Roisin's mother.

Why would they come here in the middle of the—

"The king," Lord Devon began, his shoulders slumping inside his dark coat.

My head started to shake. Numbness spread through my limbs. "Don't say it. Please." If they didn't say it, then it wouldn't be real. My father had been better. He'd told me to leave. He wouldn't have told me to go if he wasn't certain he'd last the night. And I'd . . . I'd left him all alone.

I felt Roisin's presence at my back.

Lady Seren bowed her head and said, "I'm afraid the king is dead."

14

———

ROISIN

THE KING IS DEAD.

I recognized the disbelief in Caiman's eyes, the pain shining in their dark depths. I reached for him, clutching his soft shirt, feeling as helpless as he looked.

Caiman glared at my hand until I removed it. What right did I have to comfort him after acting so foolishly for so long? I was probably the last person he needed right now. No doubt he regretted wasting this night with me instead of spending it with his father.

Not one tear fell from his black eyes as his curled shoulders straightened and his expression went blank. "Lord Devon, fetch General Newton and tell him the news. Funeral arrangements must be made with haste. There will be no wake—"

Lord Devon raised a hand. "But, your highness, it is customary—"

"I said there will be *no* wake. Arrange a meeting with the council first thing in the morning."

"Are you certain—"

"Just do it."

"Yes, your highness. Right away, your highness." Lord Devon bowed and hurried down the hall in a flurry of robes and wild red hair.

"Lady Seren, I appreciate what you did for my father," Caiman said in a much softer tone. "You are welcome to stay in the castle as long as you wish, but you may also return to Iodale if you choose."

"She can't go," I cried. Not yet. I wasn't ready. After what had happened tonight, I wasn't sure I'd ever be ready.

Caiman turned to me, and the warmth he'd afforded my mother evaporated.

"If she goes, then I'll be all alone." I'd have Lowri, but she was no replacement for my mother.

Caiman flinched as if I'd struck him.

How selfish are you, Roisin? He'd just lost his entire family, and here I was, complaining about my mother being a short journey away.

Caiman nodded once, as if coming to some sort of silent conclusion. "My father was the one who insisted we wed. With him gone, there is no longer any need for us to continue this farce. I can find another fae bride with whom to build an alliance. If you wish to return to Iodale with your mother, I will demand an immediate annulment. Decide before the coronation," he went on, shoving his hands deep into his pockets, "for once you are crowned queen, there will be no going back."

Each retreating step he took left my heart sinking lower and lower until I could barely feel it beating. Ever since I'd chosen Alrec, I'd been in training to become the next Queen of Vellana. What did I have if not that?

My mother watched Caiman until he disappeared into the king's suites at the end of the hall. "Oh, Roisin." Tears shimmered in her eyes as she took my hand and brought me back into Caiman's room. "Tell me what has happened."

Where did I begin? The past, I could learn to forgive, but this guilt felt impossible to overcome. "The thought of caring for another man feels as if I am betraying Alrec." He'd only been gone a matter of weeks. Even my closest friend thought me a traitor for softening toward Caiman.

She brushed my hair back from my face, smoothing a hand along my damp cheek. "How can you think betraying a dead man is worse than betraying yourself? I have seen the two of you together, there is something between you— something deep and true. There always has been. Why do you think I encouraged you to uphold the contract?"

How could she have seen something that wasn't there? All we'd felt for one another for years had been disdain. Perhaps some tolerance as well. But a solid relationship needed to be built on more.

If not love, at least respect and trust.

In this moment, it felt as if I couldn't even trust myself.

"I don't know if I can trust him, Mum. They say he's done terrible things."

Her lips pursed. "Like what?"

I listed the grievances Alrec and Kerrington had told me about. The time as children when Caiman had burned all of Alrec's favorite toys. When he had tried to drown Kerrington in the sea. When he had accosted a woman for stepping in front of his horse. The list went on and on.

My mother remained silent for what felt like forever, her brow slightly furrowed as she considered all I'd revealed.

"Well?" I desperately needed someone to tell me what to do. Was I was a fool for considering returning to Iodale, or was I a fool for thinking I could come to care for the man I'd married?

Which one was it?

She touched a finger to my brow. "What have you seen with these eyes?" The top of my ear. "What have you heard with these ears? What do you feel in your heart?" She pressed a hand to my chest.

"That's what scares me most of all." That Alrec may have lied to me about everything. All these years, I may have trusted—may have loved—the wrong man. How could I be certain this wasn't a mistake as well? "What if none of it was real? What if he never loved me at all?"

"Prince Alrec loved you. But I'm afraid he loved himself more."

It felt traitorous to admit it, but sometimes I'd felt the same.

"I cannot speak of the stories I don't know," she went on, "but Prince Caiman has been nothing but kind to me. To be honest, I was shocked when you picked his brother. But I respected your decision just as I will respect your decision in this."

"He's better off without me." He deserved a wife who trusted him. One who could give him her whole heart without reservation. A fresh start with someone else.

"You and I both know that's not true. He is all alone and expected to rule a nation. You are exactly the woman he needs."

Was I that woman? I wasn't so sure. But I could be.

"I always thought he despised me." And I'd been so horrible to him for so long. Could he find it in his heart to forgive me?

A small, sad smile played on my mother's lips when her eyes fell on the picnic still spread across the rug. "Midnight picnics are not the actions of a man who despises his wife."

She left me there, staring at a plateless picnic thrown

together by Caiman's own hands. He would've had to go to the kitchens to gather everything. And yet he'd done it—not because it had been expected of him but because he'd wanted to.

He'd done it for me.

Going back to Iodale felt like giving up on who I knew in my bones I was meant to be: the first fae queen of Vellana. I wanted to make a difference in this world. If Caiman married someone else, who's to say she would feel the same? Perhaps she would be content to sit on a tiny throne at his side wearing a pretty dress and a demure smile.

Was that what this country—what this alliance —needed?

I thought of Iodale and Vellana, two different islands that both felt like home.

I thought of the humans and the fae, two groups of people who had, through marriage, become my family. My responsibility.

Finally, I thought of Alrec and Caiman. Could there be room in my heart for them both?

I picked up the empty wine bottle, remembering the way I'd felt when I found Caiman knocking on my door. The relentless flutters in my stomach. The pounding of my heart. The desire coursing through my veins.

If I could learn to trust him, I knew I could love him as well.

If I could love him, perhaps he could love me in return.

15

CAIMAN

Every single counsellor wore black, making it impossible to forget that the castle was in mourning for the second time in as many months. Even Kerrington, who usually opted for bright, flashy colors, had on a black waistcoat over a black shirt. It matched the black bruises beneath his eyes from my fist.

Last night, I hadn't slept a wink, leaving me exhausted, irritable, and brewing for a fight. And if Kerrington didn't stop smirking from across the table, I was going to pick up the globe and throw it at his overlarge head. Lord Devon had tried to convince me to take today to grieve my father's passing but the last thing I wanted was to ruminate on all I'd lost.

"That is the worst idea I've ever heard," I said, delighting in the way Kerrington's face flushed. "Sending troops to invade another country is an act of war. We are lucky that my brother's stunt in Southbay didn't result in more deaths."

King Tarren's ships had returned cannon fire but had

ceased the moment the ship Alrec had commandeered was lost to the depths.

They may never compose ballads in my name or build statues celebrating my reign, but I didn't need any of those things. All I wanted was for my people to enjoy peace and prosperity. And that wouldn't happen if we went around with a chip on our shoulder, picking fights with anyone and everyone who crossed our path.

"Prince Caiman is right." Lord Devon gave his son a disappointed frown. "Our aim is to maintain peace, not start a war."

"Maintain peace?" Kerrington snorted. "Those bastards killed Prince Alrec! We should be seeking retribution, not cowering in this room."

"Prince Alrec killed himself," Broderick growled. "Did you forget that I was there? That I heard him go against a direct order from the captain and tell our men to fire upon an enemy ship?"

Kerrington jabbed an accusatory finger across the table toward where Broderick sat in my old chair. "You forget yourself, *guard*. If you were any good at your job, Prince Alrec would be here instead of you."

"Enough!" I slammed my hands against the table, delighting in the way everyone jumped in their chairs. "I'll not have you squabbling with our new emissary."

Broderick whipped toward me.

"That is, if you accept the post," I added. My original plan had been to announce the position after my coronation. Too late to worry about that now.

Broderick bowed his head. "It would be my honor, your highness."

"You cannot be serious," Kerrington scoffed. "What

does he know about being a bloody emissary? He's not even a member of the gentry."

"Broderick has followed my brother around long enough to understand the ways of polite society, he is trustworthy, and, most importantly, he knows when to keep his mouth shut."

Kerrington skulked in his chair but thankfully said no more.

"I know my father had planned on sending someone to the Black City, and now that we have our man, I will take suggestions on what our approach should be when meeting with King Tarren."

"I could draft a letter, if your highness wishes it," offered Devon. "A peace treaty of sorts. I believe it would be most prudent to prove our commitment to maintaining a positive relationship between our two nations."

"An excellent idea. How soon can we have a ship ready to sale?"

"As early as next week."

Brilliant. The sooner this matter was behind us, the better. "Broderick, does that give you enough time to get your affairs in order?"

"Plenty."

That was one of the things I liked about my guard. The man never used ten words when one would do. "Any word from our people on what Tarren's ships were doing in the bay in the first place?"

All the men shook their heads.

"That should be a priority as well. Open lines of communication are of the upmost importance."

Maybe if Roisin had communicated with me, our story could've had a happier ending.

He's the heir.

My teeth ground together. Maybe not.

Before breaking for tea, Devon insisted on discussing one final order of business: my coronation.

"I want no fanfare," I said. What would be the point? It wasn't as if this were some sort of celebration. I wanted to take the throne the same way I'd lived most of my life: in silence. "Only the necessary members of the council will be present."

Lord Devon glanced at his fellow counsellors before clearing his throat. "With all of the darkness that has clouded these past few months, Vellana needs something to celebrate. I would suggest just the opposite."

Typically, a new monarch wasn't crowned for months to give everyone time to grieve the previous one. After losing Alrec and now my father, we needed to show our allies and our enemies that we had not fallen apart. But that didn't mean we needed to throw a bloomin' party.

"Does everyone agree with Lord Devon?"

Heads bobbed from one end of the table to the other. Everyone but Kerrington's. "For once, I agree with the prince. The fewer people know he is our king, the better."

Lord Devon's face turned the same shade of red as his hair. "How dare you speak so disrespectfully of our king."

The bastard had been disrespecting me for years. I bit the inside of my cheek to keep from saying what I really wanted to. "Out of my respect for your father, I will not remove you from this council. But if you wish to keep your seat, I suggest you learn to hold your tongue."

I waited for him to bite back—hoped for it, actually. Instead, Kerrington shrank in his chair like a dog with its tail between its legs and swallowed whatever retort lived on his tongue.

Maybe being king wouldn't be so bad after all.

After the meeting, I invited Broderick to share a private lunch in the privy chamber. He sat rigidly on the chair across from me at the small table set for two, looking as uncomfortable as a nun in a bawdy house. Wine had been served—which Broderick had yet to touch. He'd eaten all of his soup, though, and was steadily making his way through the vegetables on his plate of braised beef.

"Do you have family in Vellana, Broderick?" Being an emissary required a good deal of travel that wouldn't suit a family man.

"Most of my kin hail from Airren, sire. But the majority of them have passed on."

"Airren, you say? What part?"

"Just north of Gaul."

The area north of Gaul was near the Tearmann border. "Have you ever been?"

"Once. A long time ago."

"I hear it's beautiful there." Alrec and I had never been permitted to visit. I'd have to remedy that.

"It is."

"Very different from the Black City." It was rumored that King Tarren's stronghold had been built into the side of a mountain, carved into stone as black as pitch. An impenetrable fortress that only a fool would dare to attack.

"I suppose I'll find out next week."

I set my fork aside, the food no longer appealing. What if Broderick had accepted earlier only to save face in front of the council? "You do understand that you can turn me down, and I will not be offended. But I feel your talents are wasted here. Unlike my brother, I do not need a babysitter."

He stopped eating long enough to give me a small smile.

"No, your highness. You certainly do not." His knife and fork clinked against the plate when he cut another slice of beef. "As I said earlier, it would be an honor to serve you in any capacity. If that means traveling between here and the continent, then so be it."

In a world where everything felt as though it was crumbling around me, at least one thing seemed to be going right.

"I appreciate that more than you can imagine." My first act as king, and I knew beyond a shadow of a doubt that it was the right one. If only every decision could be as simple.

Like the decision to maintain peace. I wouldn't cower once I took the throne, but I had nothing to prove to King Tarren or anyone else. If they attacked us, I would defend our people and our borders. Hopefully, it wouldn't come to that.

Broderick lifted his serviette from his lap to wipe his mouth. "Too many lives are lost over pride and greed. I will do my best to assure the king of your intentions."

"Thank you, Broderick. Your loyalty means more than you know." At least there was one person in this world who had faith in me.

16

ROISIN

I stared into the milky cup of tea, mesmerized by the way the steam danced in the air. Breakfast was the last thing I wanted, but lying in bed all day wouldn't fix things. And I desperately wanted to fix them.

I'd spent the first half of the night tossing and turning, playing Caiman's words over and over in my mind. The second half I'd spent cursing myself for not giving him the benefit of the doubt, going straight to him that very first day and demanding an explanation for his degrading remarks.

News of the king's death had rocked the castle. Black banners hung in place of the red and gold ones that normally flew from the turrets. The maids who passed wore black hoods over their hair, and the manservants had exchanged their crisp white shirts for black ones.

According to my mother, preparations for the king's funeral in two days' time were well underway. When Caiman did not come in for breakfast, I remembered he'd set a meeting with the war council for this morning.

I ate my poached eggs and toast while Lowri chatted

about what I'd wear to Caiman's coronation ceremony. I didn't have it in me to confess that I may not be attending.

When Lowri asked if I wanted to go for a walk in the gardens, I feigned a headache, retreating to my room, only to find servants carrying trunks from the bedchamber. I ran in, skidding to a halt when I saw Caiman supervising all my belongings being packed away in more trunks.

He'd made his decision. He was sending me away.

"What's happening?" I managed, even though I already knew. It was over. It was really over.

"Your things are being moved to your old chamber," he said, barely acknowledging me as the last of the servants lugged the final trunk into the hallway. "You will be staying there until you return to Iodale."

Broderick offered me a pitying look from his post in front of the window.

I tamped down my rising panic, lifting my chin as I faced my husband. "And if I do not wish to return to Iodale?"

Caiman's eyes widened, surprise flickering across his features. "I . . . um . . ." His gloved hands flexed. Shifting his weight from one foot to the other, he scanned my face. "I suppose that is your choice to make."

Wasn't he angry with me? Didn't he want to wash his hands clean of me and move on with his life?

Midnight picnics are not the actions of a man who despises his wife.

Could my mother be right?

I crossed my arms over my chest, flushing when I noticed Caiman's gaze fall to the dress's square neckline. "Are the queen's apartments ready yet?"

Caiman's jaw went slack.

Broderick hid a gruff laugh behind a more mannerly cough.

As if snapping himself out of a trance, Caiman gave his head a vigorous shake. "No."

"Oh . . ."

"What I mean is, no, they're not ready yet. But they will be. Soon. Perhaps next week?" He ran a hand through his hair. "I'm not sure. But I can find out. If you want, that is."

"Please do and let me know what they say. I look forward to occupying them once they're finished." I turned to leave, hesitating when my gaze landed on the rug where we'd sat and laughed last night. Now was as good a time as any to prove how committed I was to making this work. I twisted back around and closed the distance between us, trying to ignore the way he stiffened and the sound of his breath hitching the moment my lips met his cheek. "I am sorry that I never came to you for answers. I hope you can find it in your heart to forgive me," I said, my voice no more than a shaky whisper as I backed away and escaped to my chambers.

Lowri lounged on the chaise in my former bedroom, munching grapes as she supervised two maids transferring my garments into the armoire. I didn't recognize the taller of the two, but the shorter one, I knew.

When Falin's rich brown eyes met mine, her face flushed. Her curtsy was as atrocious as it had been that day in the garden, but her boots gleamed.

"Falin? What are you doing here? I thought you were assigned to the kitchens."

When she didn't immediately respond, the other

servant nudged Falin with her elbow. "Y-yes, your highness. But Prince Caiman . . . I mean, the new king . . . he . . . you see, he sought me out a few weeks ago and asked if I'd be interested in workin' upstairs since the pay is that bit better."

Caiman had done that? My heart melted at the subtle kindness. Although I would've liked to have known, somehow it meant so much more that he hadn't boasted about it afterward.

"Thank you for helping with my dresses, Falin."

"It's my pleasure, your highness."

Lowri looked at me as though I'd lost my mind. I stole a grape and popped it into my mouth, feeling more hopeful than I had since Alrec's death. The maids finished shortly after and flitted from the room.

Lowri poked my thigh with her long nail. "What was that about?"

"What do you mean?"

The dress I had on felt too heavy for the humid day. I snagged another grape before going to the armoire to choose a different one for the afternoon. What was Caiman's favorite color? I wanted to wear something that would make my husband stare at me the way he'd done during our picnic.

"Why did you bother speaking to those wretched humans? They're only servants."

"Servants or not, I will treat them with respect. And if you plan on remaining in Vellana, I suggest you do the same." I was about to give up my search when I found a dusty rose gown with a fitted bodice and a V at the neck deeper than any I'd dared to wear before.

"I feel like I don't even know you anymore."

The feeling is mutual.

"You used to be on our side," she said, "but now you're on theirs."

"There are no sides in this, Lowri." That was the whole point of this alliance, to erase the division between us.

"If you believe that, then you are a fool." Lowri plucked a grape from the stem. The fruit crunched between her teeth when she shoved it into her mouth.

My hands clenched on the hanger. "This is my home now, and—"

"Is it? With the prince removing you from his chambers, I'd assumed the rumors of an annulment were true. I thought we'd be going back to Iodale with your mother."

The dress slipped from my fingers. "Is that what you want?"

"There's nothing here for me, *your highness*. Not all of us have a prince to shield us from these humans and their cutting remarks."

Where was all this coming from? Not once had Lowri so much as hinted that she wished to return to our homeland. "Did something happen? You must tell me if you are having trouble again." Had I been so blinded by my own problems that I hadn't noticed my friend hurting as well?

She tore another grape free from the stem. "It's mostly Kerrington. He's changed since Alrec died."

"Why does it matter? You said you no longer cared for him."

"The man I *did* care for married another." She gave me a pointed look, eyes swimming with tears, before she lowered her head. "And when I approached Kerrington to make amends, he said he wanted nothing to do with a fickle fae."

"There are plenty of other men here." The court was full of eligible bachelors. Lords and dukes and earls. Beyond these walls was an entire swarm of men, adventurous sea captains, dashing soldiers— "What about Broderick?"

Her nose wrinkled. "You think I want to be some lowly guard's wife?"

Being the king's personal guard was an esteemed position. "Caiman respects him. He isn't hard on the eyes, and he is most loyal." Something Kerrington clearly was not.

"If you like him so much, perhaps you can marry him when the prince dies."

I hissed in a breath, my cheeks burning at the venom in her tone.

Lowri set the bowl of empty stems aside and stood, looking past me toward the door. "I came here not to live your life but to find my own. And all I've found is disappointment. I want to go home."

I watched her leave with no desire to call her back, knowing the woman I'd grown up with in Iodale wasn't the same one who had walked out the door.

17

ROISIN

CAIMAN STROLLED INTO THE DINING ROOM DEEP IN discussion with Lord Devon. When he saw me waiting for him at the head of the table, his footsteps faltered. The heat in his gaze as his dark eyes swept from my braided hair to the V in my dress left my own legs weak. Thankfully, the full chiffon skirt kept their quaking hidden from those around us.

He muttered something to Lord Devon and quickly crossed to where I stood. When I smiled, he frowned. I didn't want him to frown. I wanted him to return my smile. He caught my hand and towed me out the door, past a confused Broderick, and into one of the deep bay windows lining the breezeway.

The moment we were out of view, he let me go to tug the heavy velvet drapes closed. Lamps flickered outside in the courtyard, fighting against the falling darkness.

"What's wrong?" I asked, on the verge of tears. I had tried so hard to look well for him, and he looked as if he wanted to fight someone.

Sinking onto the wide windowsill, Caiman dropped his

head into his hands. "I cannot be in a room full of people with you looking like that."

I pressed a hand to my queasy stomach, glancing down at the shimmering material. "You don't like my dress?"

"Don't like it? You look like . . ." His cheeks flushed. "You look like the faerie from the painting."

That's why I had chosen this dress. I may not have known his favorite color, but I knew his favorite painting. And I'd asked Falin to braid flowers into my hair just like the girl Caiman had hoped I'd be.

"Is that bad?"

"Not at all. It's just . . . How am I supposed to hold a coherent conversation with anyone else when all I want to do is stare at you?"

His confession brought a blush to my own cheeks, and a nervous giggle escaped my lips. "Are we to miss dinner then?"

His brow furrowed as he considered my question with comical intensity. And then my blasted stomach moaned, ruining the moment and sending him shooting to his feet. He held up both hands as if I were a cornered animal about to bolt. "Don't . . . don't go anywhere. Please."

And then he was gone. I paced back and forth, my hands wringing my skirt and my stomach a jumble of nerves and my shoes pinching my feet. I slipped them off, hiding them in the folds of the long drapes and sighing as the cold marble soothed my soles and my soul.

A curse erupted from outside the curtains. I drew them aside, peering through the gap. Caiman lugged one of the chairs from the library while Broderick and another guard heaved a small wooden table into the alcove. A third guard appeared from around the corner carrying another chair. The men set the furniture in the alcove and drew the curtains closed, leaving us in a world of our own. Caiman pulled out a chair, waiting behind until I sat before taking his own seat.

What was I supposed to do with my hands? Folding them on top of the table made this feel like a meeting, and hiding them beneath my thighs revealed my nervousness. Caiman's back remained straight as he drummed his fingers against the pitted tabletop and stared at me with his unnerving eyes.

As much as I wanted to know how he was faring in light of his father's passing, I couldn't bring myself to ask. He'd lost so much these past few weeks, the last thing he needed was to be reminded. Tonight, I wanted him to think of something else.

I wanted him to think of me.

A moment later, a footman pushed through the curtains with a silver tray, which he left on a small stand. Beneath the tray's lid were two steaming plates of food that instantly made my mouth water. One plate had roasted potatoes dripping with butter and flecked with parsley, a mountain of carrot spears glazed with honey, and a fresh spinach salad drizzled with oil and vinegar. The second plate was identical to the first except for a few thin slices of turkey topped with lumps of deep red cranberry sauce.

Caiman set the one without the turkey in front of me and took the other for himself.

"You didn't give me any meat," I remarked, handing him a set of cutlery and a glass of wine from the tray.

He glared down at his plate, a frown tugging at his lips. "I didn't think you ate meat."

Despite living in the castle for months, the serving staff still gave me meat with every meal. I had believed no one noticed that Lowri, my mother, and I never touched the stuff.

"I don't. I just wasn't aware you knew that about the fae."

"I already told you that I did research."

"How much research exactly?"

Caiman set his cutlery aside in favor of his glass of wine. When he took a sip, his mouth pinched. "An embarrassing amount."

"And did you find answers to all your questions?"

He choked on his drink, spilling wine down the front of his white shirt. Cursing, he dragged a serviette from the tray and dabbed at the stain, his color rising.

I leaned heavily against the arm of my chair, interested in the way he avoided my gaze. "Will I take that as a no?"

His eyes flicked to me before returning to the stain. "I was curious as a boy." The tips of his rounded ears turned deep red. "I had a lot of questions."

"You can ask me anything, you know." I wanted Caiman to know me. It surprised me how much. I sliced a carrot and took a bite. Butter and rich honey burst on my tongue, tender and cooked to perfection.

He thanked me but kept his questions to himself. The sounds of cutlery on plates and the occasional clink of a glass against the tabletop were the only sounds as we finished our dinner. Caiman's gaze drifted to me almost as often as mine darted to him. He finished first, setting his dishes on the tray and topping up both our glasses with what was left of the wine.

For the first time since he'd sat down, he relaxed against the high back of the chair, one hand twisting the stem of his glass, eyes fixed on me.

"When you said you wanted to stare, I thought you were

joking." I offered a jittery laugh, gripping the edges of my chair.

"I rarely get the opportunity and want to take full advantage. Am I making you uncomfortable?" The low timbre of his voice left my heart racing.

He was, but not in the way he meant. He made me feel hot and cold and queasy but also so very excited and . . . Did this window open? I needed air before I burst into flames.

"No. I like it." Having him look at me like that made me feel like the only woman in the castle—in the kingdom.

"Do you, now?" Chewing the inside of his cheek, he tapped a gloved finger against the glass. "What else do you like?"

Heat pooled in my belly, leaving my toes curling on the marble. "What do you mean?"

"That's one of my lingering questions, something not written in any of the books I've read."

"Fae are known for their fondness for sunshine and sweets, music and dancing."

Some of his black hair slipped its queue when he shook his head. "Not the fae. I want to know about you. What do you like, Roisin?"

There was no mistaking the heat in his gaze as his eyes tracked from my lips to the lowest point of the V in my dress and back again.

"I . . . I don't know."

He finished what was left of his drink, and when he set the glass on the tray, his lips glistened.

I bet they'd taste like wine.

Caiman eased forward, leaning his elbow against the table. "I'd like to find out." He lifted his hand, as if to reach for me, then paused. "Would it be all right if I touched you?"

With my voice suddenly absent, all I could do was nod.

His brow pinched as he traced a solitary finger down the column of my throat. My eyelids fluttered closed, and I gave in to the sensations building within me. When he reached the hollow, he followed my collarbone to where the sleeve of my dress met my shoulder, hooked his finger beneath, and drew it aside. I held my breath, dying to know what he would do next.

Something warm and soft grazed my bare skin.

He'd replaced his finger with his lips, and when he kissed his way back to my throat, I threaded my fingers through his silky hair, clutching him against me, arching my back, wanting him to kiss me harder. Slower. Lower.

I forgot where we were—*who* we were. We became two people without a past or future, living in the present. A present that was beautiful and full of hope and passion. A low growl rumbled from his throat as his hands clasped my waist, kneading my ribs, working their way higher as he trailed kisses down the V of my dress.

Voices cut through the blood pounding in my ears. Caiman must've heard them as well because he stilled, dropping his forehead against my chest for a split second before bringing his mouth to my ear to whisper, "Something tells me you liked that."

The sleeve he'd removed slipped lower as my chest heaved. "Very much."

"Shall we continue this conversation in my chambers?"

"Your highness?" a deep male voice interrupted.

Cursing, Caiman twisted toward the drapes. "What the hell is it, Broderick?"

How he spoke at all was a wonder to me. I didn't have a coherent thought in my head.

"Lord Devon has asked me to remind you that you called a meeting."

"For the love of all that is holy," he muttered before saying louder, "Tell him to cancel it."

"Your highness . . ." *Lord Devon.* "With all due respect, the members of the council are gathered and waiting."

Caiman groaned, yanking on the ends of his hair.

As much as I wanted him to stay, I told him that he should go. We both needed our rest for tomorrow's funeral, and we had the rest of our lives to discover each other.

I committed to memory the obvious reluctance in his gaze and the way it felt when he dragged his leather-clad thumb across my bottom lip. Certain he was going to kiss me, I eased forward on my chair.

Sighing, he dropped his hand and pushed to his feet. "Thank you for tonight. This week has been . . . exceedingly difficult, and you helped me forget about everything. For that, I am grateful."

I huffed a laugh to conceal my growing disappointment. "Anytime you need a distraction, you know where to find me."

Caiman bent at the waist to look me in the eye. "A distraction is something that draws one's attention away from what truly matters. This dress"—he settled my fallen sleeve back in place—"is a distraction. Those infernal men waiting in the council chamber are a distraction. None of it is as important as you. And the only reason I am leaving right now is because I am not yet king and need them to think I possess some semblance of self-control." He moved closer, his heated breath tickling against my neck when he whispered, "And the only reason I am not kissing you is because if I start, I won't want to stop."

When he straightened, the breath I held escaped in an audible *woosh* as I fell back against the chair. Something told me that when Caiman finally kissed me, I wouldn't want him to stop either.

18

CAIMAN

THE HOLLOW CHAMBER AT THE BACK OF THE CHAPEL WHERE I'd been cloistered since early this morning had become a cage. Sunlight streamed through the lone stained-glass window, baking me alive. The golden cherubs carved into the mirror's frame stared at me with tiny smirks on their chubby faces as beads of sweat collected at the back of my neck, soaking the stiff collar of my shirt, all the way through to my red coat.

I shifted, wishing the garment weren't so bloomin' heavy. As if I wasn't already sweating through the ridiculous number of layers, they'd gone and added another one, a mantle lined with fur. Surely there had to be a lighter option. I'd be lucky to make it through the ceremony without keeling over from heat stroke. The gold medallions draped around my neck weren't helping the matter, and all the gold weapons on my belt left me walking like a man with wooden legs.

I didn't consider myself a vain man by any means, but I looked ridiculous.

"It's time, your highness," Broderick called from the

doorway, his gold and red dress uniform similar to my own. Only he didn't look ready to pass out.

I didn't give a whit about any of the noblemen or dignitaries crowded into the wooden pews. The whole chapel could be empty for all I cared—save for one person. I tried to look past the guard, but all I saw was an empty stone hallway. "Where's Roisin?"

I'd asked the same question on the morning of our wedding, certain she'd abandon me at the altar.

Broderick gave me a knowing smile. "She is waiting for you."

My heart leapt.

Waiting for me.

No one else.

Me.

I knew better than to believe her decision to remain married had anything to do with wanting to be my wife. And yet, knowing she would be by my side made what was to come a little more bearable.

The dinner we'd shared together last week had given me hope that we could have a real relationship. And perhaps someday, a real marriage. And it had given me a long, restless night dreaming of an ethereal woman with silver hair in a pink dress. The fact that she'd gone to so much trouble to match her outfit to the painting, even down to the tiny flowers in her hair, left my heart swelling.

I walked stiffly into the small hallway, the heavy mantle dragging every step of the way. My lungs started to ache. I needed air that didn't smell like dust and stones.

And then Roisin stepped into view, and the ache slid lower.

Although she'd been a vision in ivory silk and lace on

our wedding day, she'd hidden herself and her misery beneath a veil.

Today, there was no veil. And she didn't appear miserable.

She looked happy.

It probably has nothing to do with you, I reminded myself. She was about to be crowned Queen of Vellana. Why wouldn't she be happy?

The gold ribbon criss-crossed at the center of her gown highlighted her trim waist, the soft swell of her hips. The straight neckline came off her shoulders. When I wet my lips, I swear I could taste the unique blend of magic and sunlight that I'd sampled the other night.

"Roisin, you look . . ."

"Sweaty?" She dashed a hand at her brow, then relocated her braid from where it fell down her spine to across her right shoulder.

"I can assure you that you are nowhere near as sweaty as I am." Probably not the most polite of compliments, but it made her giggle. I tugged on the front of my buttoned coat in an attempt to flush some air against my skin. "You'd think with all the gold in the kingdom's coffers we'd be able to afford some appropriate clothing."

Her eyes lit up like sparklers when she grinned. "You'd think."

The priest announced us in a booming baritone that echoed off the vaulted ceilings.

I held out a hand, stunned when she took it without hesitation and waited for me to lead her into the chapel. Red roses embellished the arched windows, and garlands surrounded the door frames. Candelabras flickered at even intervals on either side of the rectangular room.

The entire congregation stood and remained standing

until we reached the stretch of red carpet beneath the rosette windows. Lord Devon and the rest of the advisory committee filled the front pews, along with Roisin's mother and Lowri. The rest of the faces became a hazy blur.

When Roisin let my hand fall, I resisted the urge to cling to her—to cling to anything but the heavy air hanging over me.

On the altar next to the priest sat the tools for today's coronation. There'd be the usual festivities afterward, banquets and balls and eventually a tour around the country.

All of it felt contrived.

These people didn't know me the way they'd known Alrec.

And they certainly didn't care for me.

I'd been crowned by default. A runner-up.

Always the second choice.

The priest held out his hands, bringing them down in a fluid motion. The congregation sat in unison. "Lords and ladies gathered here today, I present to you Caiman Joseph Howard I, your undoubted king. From this day forward, do you swear homage and fealty to him as your ruler?"

Echoes of agreement lifted around us.

The priest turned to me, offering no hint of a smile. "Will you solemnly swear to govern the peoples of Vellana, Airren, Alba, and any future territories according to their respective laws and customs?"

I heard the words. Understood their meaning. But my tongue had swollen, and I couldn't form a response.

Until Roisin's fingers brushed against mine.

I wasn't on my own in this. She would be by my side.

"I solemnly swear so to do."

He gave a slight nod of approval. "Will you solemnly

swear to keep law and justice, in mercy, in making all your judgements?"

This time I didn't hesitate. "I will."

I may not have been the first choice as king, just as I hadn't been Roisin's first choice for a husband, but I would do my best to serve and protect my citizens and my queen.

My eyes met Roisin's, and I swore she glowed.

The priest climbed atop a small wooden stool to place another mantle across my shoulders, fastening the front with yet another gold brooch. Sweat ran like a river down my spine.

On my right ring finger, he placed a thick golden ring inlaid with rubies that my father had worn for as long as I could remember. The symbol of my "marriage" to this country and the neighboring islands. He handed me a scepter to symbolize my authority and a golden orb to represent our world. One trinket for each hand.

Now for the last and final step.

The crown.

One my father had worn, and his father before him, and his father before that. Forged of gold with pearl-lined arches bisecting in the center beneath a ruby-studded fleur-de-lis. The band at its base was inlaid with precious gems of all colors, finishing off at a line of white and black fur.

The thing was hideous.

The priest bowed his head to recite a prayer over the crown.

I felt myself sway, my arms beginning to ache with the way I'd been forced to hold the trinkets. If he didn't get on with it, I'd be flat on my back seeing stars.

He finished, climbing the single step once more and holding the crown aloft over me. "On this day a crown of gold rests upon your head, may your royal heart be so enriched and your soul be blessed with all kingly virtues."

The weight of the crown and all it represented left me frozen in place.

"All hail the king!"

I'm not yours, the crown seemed to whisper.

"All hail the king!"

You are not worthy.

"All hail the king!"

Thief. Murderer.

The priest called Roisin forward, and she stepped into the vacant space to my right, smiling for the crowd. Her promises were the same; not once did she falter. And when the man crowned her as queen consort, the crowd gave their resounding approval with an ear-splitting, "All hail the queen."

We led the procession down the steps, through the pews, to the main door, and out into the baking sun. A line of soldiers waited on either side of the path, swords lifted, forming an archway between the chapel and the castle.

A few more steps, and we'd be inside.

A few more steps, and the prying eyes would go away.

A few more steps, and the riotous cheers would fall silent.

Then the doors to the castle swung open, revealing another wave of cheers, this time from the staff, standing tall and proud in red and gold livery.

Roisin nodded and smiled at them all.

If only I could rid myself of the quiet desperation building in my chest.

I'd made a mistake.

I couldn't do this.

I couldn't be king.

19

ROISIN

I stood at the foot of the dais with the rest of the buzzing crowd, waiting for the new king to take his place at the head of the ballroom. Where there used to be three gold thrones, there were now only two. One large with an eagle's head carved at the top, the other smaller with carved roses.

One of the last gifts Alrec had given me before he'd died.

My stomach churned like I'd drunk too much wine. How could I feel even a modicum of happiness when he would never again feel anything? *You didn't die too*, I reminded myself. *You deserve to live.*

"Where is he?" Lowri hissed, a glass of champagne dangling between her fingers. Her expression grew more sour by the minute.

I hadn't seen Caiman since he'd been dragged away by Kerrington's father after the coronation ceremony. The crowd at my back grew restless, their laughter and chatter echoing off the double-height ceiling.

"I'm sure he will be here soon." After sweating through the heavy velvet dress I'd been forced to wear earlier, I'd been allowed to change into something more suitable for the weather: a burnished gold gown with a shimmering lace overskirt. The straight neckline was a bit boring, but the way the sleeves hung off my shoulders made up for it. I thought of the way Caiman's lips had felt against my skin, so warm and soft, and shivered.

Lowri swiped her forehead with a gloved hand. "I can't wait to return to Iodale where there is a breeze."

I didn't feel the expected pang of sadness at the idea of Lowri's departure. Instead, I felt almost relieved.

"Pardon me, your majesty?"

A thin young woman, not much older than myself, with rich black curls, dipped in a low curtsy. When she rose, I sucked in a breath. Her eyes were the most unusual shade of violet. I checked her ears for a tell-tale point, but they were rounded. She may have been human, but I'd bet she had fae blood somewhere in her ancestry.

She kept her hands folded in front of her, the picture of subservience. "You summoned me?"

"You must be mistaken. I haven't summoned anyone."

Doubt flickered through her eyes as her lips pursed. "I received a letter written by your own hand."

The only letter I sent was to— "What is your name?"

"Lady Whitney Frederickson, your majesty."

This was Lady Whitney? No wonder Caiman and Alrec had quarrelled over her. She had to be one of the most beautiful humans I'd ever seen.

Although no one but Lowri seemed to be paying us any attention, I didn't want anyone overhearing our discussion.

"Come with me." When Lowri made to follow, I told her this was a private conversation. Although her eyes flashed, she didn't protest, instead catching another glass of champagne from a passing servant. Lady Whitney followed me to an alcove behind the deep red curtains draped on either side of the dais, near the hidden door used only by the royal family and close friends.

With all that had happened, I had completely forgotten about sending that letter.

"This is terribly awkward," I began, straightening to my full height to meet her gaze head-on, "but I have a few questions of a delicate nature."

A small smile played on her lips. "You wish to know about my relationship with your husband."

I could only nod, not trusting my voice to remain steady.

"Now that his brother is gone, I suppose there is no longer a reason for me to keep my secret," she said almost hesitantly, eyes downcast toward her pink slippers. "Caiman and I used to be friends. His brother grew jealous of our closeness. He couldn't fathom why I would care for Caiman over him."

I had a sinking feeling I knew where this conversation was headed.

Lady Whitney shifted from one foot to the other, clenching and unclenching her skirts.

"Go on," I encouraged, needing to hear the rest of it even though my heart already ached.

"Prince Alrec kissed me without my permission. When I tried to stop him, he grew more insistent. Caiman found us and kept things from going further. To keep him quiet, Prince Alrec . . . he did unspeakable things. By the time Caiman was released from the infirmary, the issue had been dealt with."

"Dealt with how?"

Her hands shook as she wrung them together. "I do not wish to speak ill of the previous king, but he was blind to his eldest son's true nature." Tears gathered along her dark lashes. "Prince Alrec threatened me and my family, saying I had to go along with his account or suffer the consequences. I didn't want to, but Caiman told me it was for the best."

Heavens above, I had been as blind as the king. I pressed my palm to my spinning head. What a fool I'd been. All this time . . .

Lord Kerrington appeared from around the drapes, a glass of faerie wine in each hand. The green jacket and waistcoat he wore matched his eyes. When he saw Lady Whitney, his face lost its color. "What the hell is she doing here?"

Lady Whitney stumbled back.

"You forget yourself, Kerrington," I snapped.

His eyes narrowed as he bowed his head mockingly. "My apologies, *your majesty*. But you must understand my shock at seeing you conversing with a traitor."

He wouldn't speak so horribly of the poor woman if he knew the truth. "Lady Whitney is—"

A hand curled around my arm. I met Lady Whitney's pleading gaze. This wasn't my story to tell. It was hers. And for some reason, she appeared ashamed by it even though she had done nothing wrong.

"Lady Whitney is here as my personal guest. You'd do well to remember that." I gave her hand a reassuring squeeze, letting her know I meant every word. "It was a pleasure meeting you. I do hope to see more of you while you are visiting, Lady Whitney."

She blinked back tears. "It would be my pleasure, your highness."

"Please, go and enjoy yourself. And if you have any trouble"—I scowled at Kerrington—"do not hesitate to come to me with your grievances."

Whitney bobbed a curtsy, giving Kerrington a wide berth as she returned to the festivities.

Kerrington drank both glasses of wine, one after the other. "With all due respect," he drawled, wiping his mouth on his sleeve, "you must be careful of those you allow close to your person now that you are queen. Lady Whitney is a conniving little witch, desperate to align herself with power at any cost."

I was through having other people tell me who someone was or was not. From now on, I would be making my own decisions. And I liked Lady Whitney, so Kerrington could sod off. "Did you need something else, Lord Kerrington?"

The murmuring crowd on the other side of the curtain grew louder. The musicians couldn't start until the king officially arrived, and without dancing, guests turned to drink. Drink that had been flowing like water for well over an hour.

"What I need is for our stone king to get his arse out here so we can get on with this *celebration*."

The sarcasm in Kerrington's tone was impossible to ignore. "Do my ears deceive me? I was certain I heard you speak harshly about your king."

"We need King Caiman, *your majesty*," he amended before twisting and stalking back to the eager crowd.

Where in the world was Caiman? Instead of fighting against the crowd, I headed for the secret chamber that Caiman had used on our wedding night. He could be anywhere. I'd start with his rooms, then the privy chamber, then the library. Inside the dark room, my eyes took a moment to adjust. When they did, I saw a figure sitting on a bench under the window, moonlight playing on his raven hair.

"There you are. Everyone is looking for—"

His head lifted. Were those tears glistening in his eyes?

"What's wrong?" I rushed. "Has something happened?"

"I do not wish to be king," Caiman muttered, dropping his head into his hands.

I crossed the tiled floor to where he sat, unsure of what to say until I stopped in front of him and his glistening eyes raised to mine. Perhaps I didn't need to say a thing.

This man had lost his brother and his father, and now he was expected to lead a nation. The weight of that burden must have been unbearable. I threaded my fingers through his hair, hugging him to my chest. His arms came around my hips, pulling me between his knees, clinging to me as if I were the sole force keeping him from breaking.

"You will be a great king," I told him, meaning every single word.

His hold on me tightened. "It shouldn't be me. It should be Alrec. This life isn't mine. It was meant for him."

"Alrec is gone." Gone and never coming back. Was I to be in love with a ghost for the rest of my life? After learning his true nature, how could I claim to love him at all? "He was . . . he was never really there."

Caiman sat up straighter, bringing his hands to cup my jaw, the buttery leather of his gloves grazing my bottom lip. "You tasted like strawberries," he whispered, stroking slowly.

I was so focused on his fingers that the words took a moment to register. "I haven't eaten any strawberries."

"Not today. Four years ago. By the pond."

"You remember?"

His thumb stilled in the center of my lip. "I've tried to forget, but the taste of you still haunts me. I wonder . . ." His hand dropped, and he eased forward until his breath mingled with mine. "I wonder what you taste like now."

I closed the distance between us, brushing my lips

against his, soft as a whisper. A memory. He made a noise low in his throat, somewhere between a groan and a growl. Full of want. Full of need. Need that I felt spreading from my core as Caiman's tongue slid along the seam of my lips, sinking inside, stealing my breath. My thoughts. A piece of my heart.

And when he drew back to gaze up at me, pupils blown wide, my chest swelled with the same wonder and hope I saw on his face. It wasn't enough. I wanted more. *Needed* more.

I shoved him back against the cushion, climbed onto his lap, and slammed my lips to his.

The taste of him filled the well of longing inside of me, stealing my guilt and grief, replacing it with something warm and sweet. Something that had a name. A name I didn't dare say aloud.

I clung to him, losing myself in the kiss and the way his hands tangled in my hair. Raked down my spine. Gripped my thighs. Like he wanted to touch me anywhere and every-where. Why had I fought this for so long? Every day I hadn't kissed him felt like a day wasted.

Caiman pressed down on my hips at the same time he raised his, and the sensation of feeling him against me made my head spin and left me gasping. He made that noise again. I felt it rumble against my chest and—

A throat cleared. "If the two of you are quite finished, the crowd is growing restless."

Kerrington had finally found us.

"*Get out,*" Caiman growled.

"You need to—"

"I said get out!"

The door slammed. Caiman cursed, his head falling back against the window. I managed to catch my breath enough to say, "He's right. This really isn't the time or place for us to . . ." My face flushed at the thought of where this had almost led.

Caiman lifted his hips again. "To what?"

I smacked his shoulder. "You know what."

His dark eyes sparkled. "You dare strike your king?"

If we didn't have an entire ballroom waiting for us, I'd have done more than strike him. I'd rip his clothes from his body and give the rumor mill something good to gossip about. "How else am I to keep you in line?"

"I can think of a few ways."

"Stop that."

"Stop what?"

"You know what," I laughed.

Groaning, Caiman scrubbed a hand down his face. It took a moment to fix the layers of my skirts until they fell just right. My husband still hadn't moved. "Your people are waiting, my king."

"I am fairly confident they would rather wait than see me in my current state," he muttered, adjusting the front of his breeches.

My face burned, and I found myself grateful for the cover of darkness. "Just . . . Um . . . Let me know when you're ready."

A chuckle. "I'm more than ready."

I stifled my giggle behind my hand, feeling lighter than I had since the day I'd lost Alrec. "You know I meant ready to go into the ballroom."

Caiman stood, straightening his breeches once more before pulling on his coat and fastening his decorative sword at his hip. "Let's get this over with."

"Just a minute. You're crooked."

He arched his brows.

"Your jacket, you rake." The lapels of his red jacket, trimmed in gold, felt velvety soft as I flattened them into place. If only my hair was as easy to fix. I brushed the bits that had escaped back from my face, but my fingers kept getting caught in the tangles. "My hair's a mess, isn't it?"

Caiman tried to help, but I had a feeling he only made it worse. "The entire kingdom is bound to know what we've been up to."

My hands fell to my sides. "Good."

A crooked grin hooked the corner of his lips as he laced his fingers with mine. "Good."

I had seen him smirk, scowl, and sneer, but I'd never seen him genuinely smile. He had such a beautiful smile, hesitant and sweet.

A herald announced our arrival, and the crowd let out a riotous cheer. Still holding hands, Caiman and I ascended the dais set up at the end of the ballroom. Glasses were raised in toast, wishing us a long and happy reign. My feet ached from the stiff velvet slippers. I swore they sighed when I landed on the red tufted cushion on my much smaller throne.

The musicians began to play, and those without partners cleared the dance floor for those itching to dance. Women in colorful dresses lined up on the left side. Men, most of them in black, formed a line opposite them.

Caiman smiled at me again before turning to watch the festivities.

When a servant brought us drinks, Caiman took one sip, made a face, and left the goblet on the tray beside him. All this happiness made me want to drink the entire glass—until I recalled our wedding night. I didn't want to drown myself in drink. I wanted to remember every moment. Every stolen glance. Every kiss.

And everything else that may or may not happen when the party ended.

The thought left my cheeks ablaze.

I glanced at my husband to find him watching me, the same heat in his gaze that I'd seen in the chamber. He waved at Broderick, and the guard came over, bending so that Caiman could whisper in his ear. Whatever he said left Broderick hurrying down the stairs to cut through the crowd.

I shifted on the cushion, my bottom already aching. "Would it be possible to get a new throne? One that isn't so—"

"Small?" Caiman finished with a smirk.

"I was going to say uncomfortable, but now that you mention it, there is quite a difference between yours and mine." I didn't want to sound ungrateful, but I just couldn't get past it. "I understand that it is customary for the king's throne to be the largest; however, it would be nice if mine were a *little* bigger."

Caiman nodded. "Consider it done."

"Just like that?"

He shrugged. "We are both to rule this country. Why wouldn't our thrones be the same?"

I found my glass and took a drink, turning his words over in my mind. "You truly wish for me to rule by your side?"

"I certainly do not want to do it on my own." He sipped his drink, made another face, and returned the glass to the tray. "There is a meeting with the council next week. Would you like to attend?"

"I would love to. That would give me the chance to broach the subject of my plans for a charity to help citizens like Falin who are struggling." The orphans and unwed mothers, women and children who seemed to have been forgotten by the world. "We could teach them skills. Help find employment and affordable housing. Most importantly, we would keep them safe and give them hope."

"It sounds like you've given this a good deal of thought."

"I have."

"I can't wait to hear more about it." From the dancefloor, I noticed Broderick waving. Caiman stood, holding out his hand. "But first, will you dance with me?"

I slipped my fingers through his, the leather of his gloves soft as petals on a rose. "I would love to."

The people blocking our path parted, allowing us through. The fast reel came to an abrupt halt, to the protest of those participating. When they saw us waiting, the floor quickly cleared.

The cello player began a slow, haunting song I remembered from my childhood, a faerie waltz.

"I love this song," I confessed, holding on to his shoulder.

Caiman's hand slipped to the small of my back and he held me close, closer than he should've considering every eye in the room was trained on us. "I thought you might."

Some of the people in the front of the crowd frowned, but most smiled sly smiles. Lowri and Kerrington wore matching glares from the bay window. My mother winked at me from beside the champagne fountain.

I must've stepped on his toes at least a dozen times, but he never once complained or called me clumsy. He just kept moving, leading me around the dancefloor. I'd never seen him dance before and had assumed he'd be terrible.

"Why don't you dance?" I asked, struggling to catch my breath.

"What do you call this?"

My hair tickled my bare shoulders when I shook my head. "We've had countless balls, and you didn't dance at any of them. I thought you'd be shocking."

"Just because I choose not to do something doesn't mean I'm not good at it." The low confession left goosebumps across my skin. "You're the only woman I've kissed, and I think I figured it out just fine."

My eyes flew to where Lady Whitney sipped champagne between two elderly women near the balcony. "You've never kissed anyone else?"

"I never wanted to."

"Really?" I had kissed other men besides Alrec. Not many, but a few. And I knew for a fact that Alrec had been unruly in his younger years. "You were never tempted?"

"I never said that."

Had he been tempted to kiss Lady Whitney? I couldn't bring myself to ask.

"Every time a certain silver-haired fae came to the castle, I found myself incredibly tempted. Unfortunately for me, she was engaged to someone else."

The song ended, and he led me through the cheering crowd to the foot of the dais where a servant waited for us with two fresh glasses of champagne. Caiman removed both from the gold tray and handed me one before leaning in close. "As soon as it is appropriate to leave, I plan on stealing you away from all these people and picking up where we left off." He straightened and took a sip of champagne, dark eyes burning through mine. "Does my queen have any objections?"

I drank the whole lot, the bubbles fizzing in my throat. "Far be it for me to go against my king's wishes."

Lord Kerrington asked me to dance next. I didn't particularly want to but knew the night would go faster if I kept moving. My heart leapt in my chest as I watched Caiman walk through a gauntlet of beautiful women, paying them no attention whatsoever.

You're the only woman I've kissed . . .

There was something sacred about the confession. Knowing the intimate moments we would share had been shared with no one else.

Kerrington took my hand, settling it on his shoulder. "You look different."

"Do I?"

The music began, slow at first before picking up pace.

"Don't tell me you're falling for our stone king. Are fae hearts truly so fickle?"

My steps stilled. The couples closest to us swerved, barely avoiding a collision. My heart was not fickle. It had been broken and betrayed and was only now beginning to heal. "I loved Alrec."

"From the way you were kissing his brother, it would appear otherwise."

I pulled my hand free. "What takes place between my husband and me is none of your concern."

"Best have a care, my queen," Kerrington murmured. "The heartless block of granite you married is willing to crush anyone who gets in his way."

"It's you who should take care, Lord Kerrington. Your queen is willing to do the same."

I left him gawking in the middle of the floor, darting between dancing couples, through the buzzing crowd, and out into the much quieter hall.

Courtiers tucked into alcoves shared whispers. Couples kissed in the shadows. Flickering candlelight from the wall sconces reflected off abandoned glasses of champagne on the windowsills.

How dare Kerrington say such horrible things to me. I'd thought we were friends. He should be supporting my decisions, or at least trying to understand them. Another foolish mistake. It was beginning to feel like the only person I could rely on was my husband.

Quick footsteps at my back left me whirling, expecting to see Kerrington.

Instead, I found my husband. "Is everything all right?"

It wasn't, but having him near made me forget about everything else. I caught his collar, dragging him forward to sample the champagne still lingering on his tongue. His fingers threaded in my hair, holding me as close as our bodies would allow.

Are fae hearts truly so fickle?

Kerrington's accusation struck like a blow to the heart. Did Caiman think me fickle as well? The backs of my eyes burned with unshed tears.

When I stepped back, Caiman refused to release me. "Roisin, what's wrong?"

"I'm sorry." I dashed at the tears falling down my cheeks. "I don't even know why I'm crying."

Liar.

Hadn't I learned the consequences of keeping such things to myself? "It's Alrec," I confessed, hating the way he stiffened at the sound of his brother's name. "I feel as if I am betraying him."

Caiman's arms came around my back, gently cradling me against his chest as if I would shatter to pieces. "Shhh, it's all right. I know how much you loved him."

I breathed him in, stealing his steadiness and strength. "I loved the man I thought he was. I don't think I'll ever stop."

A sigh. "I don't mind sharing your heart as long as there is a little room left for me."

He wasn't demanding I renounce my love for his brother or insisting I put him out of my mind. Somehow, he'd said the exact words I needed to hear.

"There is," I whispered against his lips, ready for what came next.

His answering smile made it hard to kiss him properly. When he drew away, I murmured my protest. A protest that quickly became a laugh when he swept me into his arms and carried me to our room.

20

CAIMAN

Roisin snuggled closer to me, her skin warm and soft. If I died now, I'd die with a smile on my face. There was still so much work we needed to do, on ourselves and on our relationship, on processing our grief and all we'd lost, but after a week of growing closer, I could see her island now from my bridge. And she could see mine.

Speaking of islands, I figured we should do some traveling, escape this castle and see Vellana together. Perhaps I'd speak to Lord Fisher about moving up the royal tour. Roisin would love the small palace in Shippensberg and the walled cottage in Treek. I wanted her to see every province—every village—in the kingdom she would help me rule.

Roisin's silver hair spread across the pillowcase like strands of moonlight. Cheeks flushed. Lips a dusky rose. Tanned skin seeming to glow with whatever light of magic lived within her.

Now that I had her in my bed, I never wanted her to leave.

There was a chance she may still wish to keep to her own chambers, but I sincerely hoped I had more than convinced her that sharing mine would be a far better choice.

Smiling a sleepy smile, Roisin pressed a tender kiss to my neck as she nuzzled closer, throwing one leg over mine. My hideous hands looked like an abomination where they rested on the swell of her smooth hip. She hadn't seemed to mind them last night. The memory left my stomach tightening

"Good morning, wife." I'd never tire of saying that word. *Wife*. The way it rolled off the tongue. The accompanying pang of desire.

"Morning, husband." The greeting may have been whispered against my throat, but I felt it burrow into my heart and sing to my very soul.

I was the luckiest man in the entire world. Not just for marrying this entrancing woman but for the opportunity to make a life with the only woman I had ever loved. A future filled with joy and happiness. There'd be tough times as well, but I figured after the road we'd traveled to get to this point, fate owed us a break.

She's not meant to be yours.

I buried the reminder deep inside the well of grief and guilt, which I could forget existed as long as Roisin remained near.

"How are you?" I asked.

Her back arched as she stretched in one slow, languid motion. "Hungry. And you?"

I nipped her earlobe, relishing her soft sigh and the way her short nails bit into my arm. "Starving."

Someone rapped on the door. For once in my life, couldn't I just bask in paradise before the world intervened?

"Your highness?" *Broderick.*

"That man has the worst timing," I groaned. From this day forward, I was not to be disturbed between the hours of ten and ten unless it was a matter of life or death. I'd make a royal decree. I could do that now that I was king, couldn't I?

Cursing, I fell back onto my pillow and scrubbed my hands down my face. "What is it, Broderick?"

Roisin smacked my shoulder. "Don't make the poor man shout through a door. Let him inside."

I sat up, bracing my forearms against my raised knees before tugging the covers up and over Roisin's head, earning a giggle. As much as I loved seeing her undressed, Broderick would not have the same luxury. "Come in."

Broderick opened the door and stepped inside, having the good sense to keep his gaze on his pristine black boots. "Forgive the intrusion, sire. But everyone is assembled, and the captain has informed me that the tides are favorable this morning."

Captain? Tides? Hold on. That was *today*? "Forgive me. I've been a little distracted." Roisin poked me in the side from beneath the tent of sheets. "We'll be there in ten minutes."

The moment the door closed, Roisin tossed the quilt aside. "Actually, make it twenty," I shouted, catching her by the hips and dragging my giggling wife back to bed.

I filled my lungs with restorative sea air as the last of the ship's supplies were loaded. Across the dock, Roisin hugged her mother, their words lost to the sound of water slapping the ship's hull and the screeching caw of the gulls perching on the towering masts. A two-day voyage would bring Broderick and the small party of soldiers to the port in Tivelle. From there, it would be another two days on horseback before he reached the Black City. After a brief stopover, the captain would sail for Iodale to return Lady Seren and Lady Lowri to their homes.

I expected to feel a pang of jealousy at seeing the ship I'd planned to escape on finally ready to set sail without me. But for once in my life, I had no longing to be anywhere but here.

Beside me, Broderick toyed with the hilt of his sword, his boots shifting on the wooden dock. "Is something amiss?" I asked.

His lips flattened as he stared toward the horizon, where another ship was sailing out of port, billowing white sails catching the strong breeze. "I am nervous, your highness."

"You? Nervous?" The man was made of steel. "Whatever for?"

"The last time I set foot aboard a ship, it did not end well."

Of course. How could I fault him for not wanting to go after the trauma of that day? Someone else could be appointed to his position. Maybe Lord Devon would have a few suggestions. Although such a delay could be detrimental to our efforts. "If you wish to step down as emissary—"

"I don't."

I didn't bother hiding my relief, earning a rare smile from my former guard. "Fear not. In a matter of days, you will be back on solid ground." The wind tugged at my hair, loosening some of the strands and whipping them across my cheeks.

Fishermen in tiny boats bobbed in the bay, searching for their next great haul. One of the crewmen in a loose white shirt bellowed for passengers to board. Another two scurried up the ship's rigging toward the tied sails.

Broderick bobbed his head once, his hand falling to his

side before he bowed his head. "I will make you proud, my king."

"I know you will, Broderick."

He stopped to say something to my wife before climbing the gangplank. I turned and nearly rammed into my newly appointed guard, a dour-faced man twice my age with hawk-like features and eyes that never stopped scanning our surroundings.

Lady Lowri sauntered to the edge of the dock, dropping to a low curtsy when she reached me. "King Caiman."

Roisin sidled up next to me, tears spilling through her long, dark lashes.

"Queen Roisin," she added with obvious reluctance.

Roisin's shoulders stiffened. "Goodbye, Lowri."

I wasn't sorry to see Lowri go. If only she'd take Kerrington away as well. "Will you miss her?" I asked once she'd boarded.

"I will miss the girl I once knew," Roisin said, "not the one she's become."

I wanted to ask what she meant by that but didn't have the chance before Lady Seren approached, her smile as warm and welcoming as ever. She hugged her daughter once more, both of them sobbing, murmuring words of love. She let Roisin go, kissed her cheek, then stepped over to me.

"Take care of my daughter."

"I will. I promise."

She hugged me and whispered, "And let her take care of you."

Roisin dabbed at her eyes with a handkerchief as we waved goodbye and watched the ship sail away on the morning tide. How difficult this must be for her, being left behind to rule a foreign land. Even the prize of a crown didn't seem like enough when I thought of all she had given up to remain here with me.

She was never meant to be yours.

Thief.

Murderer.

The vile words beat like a war drum in my mind while acid churned in my gut. This happiness. This promise. This hope. All of it built on my brother's grave.

I stared at the sea that had claimed Alrec's life, knowing I didn't deserve any of it.

That afternoon, I suggested a visit to the gardens to take Roisin's mind off things. When I glanced over my shoulder, I found the new guard a few paces behind us, hand on the hilt of his sword. "What do you think of my new guard?" I whispered.

She stole a look at him, quickly hiding her grimace behind a smile. "He seems a nice enough fellow," she said under her breath.

Guards weren't hired because they were nice but because they were trained killers. I decided not to mention it. "Excellent. Because I'm assigning him to you."

She halted next to a bush full of droopy pink flowers. The guard stopped as well, maintaining his distance. "Oh, please don't do that. His eyes bounce inside his head like marbles."

"Right? Do you think they're loose or something?"

She snorted, covering her grin with her hand. A moment later, she had sobered enough to continue walking down the path toward the fishpond. "We really shouldn't poke fun at him for something he obviously cannot control."

"We really shouldn't. Do you think he does it in his sleep?"

"Caiman."

"No, no, you're right. My apologies. Although he does stomp."

"Dreadfully stompy."

"I miss Broderick already."

"So do I."

We reached the final hedge before the pond, and I told the guard he could wait here. The man's head swivelled, scanning this way and that, before he nodded and said to call if we needed assistance.

A red-and-white-striped blanket was spread across the bank of the pond, a large basket overflowing with food left at the center to keep it from blowing away.

"You planned this?" Roisin asked with a devastating smile.

Having anticipated how upset she'd be after saying goodbye this morning, I'd asked her maid Falin to organize a picnic for when we returned. "You're always in a better mood when you're fed."

Laughing, she fell onto the blanket. I knelt next to her, flipping open the basket's lid. "A much better picnic than the last one, is it not? Look. Plates. Serviettes. There's even butter. And these scones don't look stale."

Roisin took each item from me, spreading them in front of us like a feast. "I don't know. I kind of enjoyed the last one."

So did I. The first part, anyway.

We ate and chatted about nothing of consequence. Being here with her, I could almost forget the mountain of duties that awaited us back at the castle and pretend we were simply two people getting to know one another.

Learning to fall in love.

Who was I kidding? I'd been in love with Roisin since the moment we met.

"No fishing today?" I teased, tossing crumbs from what remained of our scones into the grass for the birds.

"I don't believe the Vellanian queen should be caught with her skirts tied between her knees, waist-deep in a fishpond."

"Why not?"

Although she shrugged, I recognized the longing glance she cast toward the glassy pond. If the queen wanted to fish, then she should fish. Who would see her, anyway, besides me? The birds and clouds and bees? I unbuckled my boots, setting them aside and rolling my socks together on the corner of the blanket.

I stood and started for the water, sucking in a breath when my toes sank between green lily pads into the icy muck. A dragonfly whizzed past my ear. Beneath the water, flashes of gold and white darted this way and that.

"Are you mad? Caiman, you're the king," Roisin called from the shore.

"That's right. I am the king. And if anyone takes issue with me fishing in my own pond, then I will have them thrown in the stocks."

"So you are to be a tyrant then?" she asked on a laugh.

"If need be."

I stuck my hands in the water the way I'd watched Roisin do twice now. I could see fish, but the closest one was more than an arm's length away.

"You're not doing it right," she announced.

"I'm doing exactly what you've done." Hands in the water, wait, catch a fish. Simple.

"You need to stand still. That's not still, Caiman. I can

see you wiggling your fingers. Just—" Roisin made an indignant sound. "Just let me show you."

A moment later, she stood at my side, hands on her hips and an assessing tilt to her pointed chin. "First, take off the gloves."

I removed my gloves and tossed them onto the shore with a wet splat.

"Now, bend over and hold still."

"I recall telling you the same thing just this morning."

She splashed me.

"You dare attack your king?" I splashed her back, soaking her pink bodice. "Careful, or my wobbly-eyed guard may come for your head."

Roisin lunged, her cold, wet hands catching my neck and legs wrapping around my hips. "You will never catch a fish now."

"Silly wife." I caught her damp lip between my teeth. "I was never trying to catch a fish. I was trying to catch a fae."

ROISIN

With all the fluttering in my stomach, I couldn't quite catch my breath. Behind me, Caiman cursed as he fastened the buttons on my red day dress. He was still useless at tying laces, but untying them—

My face flushed.

"I could just call for Falin," I said for the third time. If he didn't hurry it on, we were going to be late for my very first council meeting. I needed them in good humor if I wanted them to approve the proposal for my charity that Caiman had helped me draft last night.

He'd been so wonderful, listening quietly as I explained my ideas, waiting until the end to offer a few suggestions of his own, as well as tips on raising the necessary funds.

"Quiet. I've almost got it." He tugged the back near my neck. "There. All finished." He stood and collected his waistcoat from where I'd discarded it an hour earlier.

I tucked the lace from my shift beneath the square neckline, examining my reflection to make sure everything was perfect. Had I made the right choice wearing my hair down, or should I have let Falin style it up? "I still don't understand why you insist on doing this yourself."

He stuffed his feet into his boots, fastening the golden buckles at the top much quicker than he'd done my buttons. "Because there may come a time when we find ourselves without assistance, and it would do no good to have my wife traipsing around the gardens with her bits on display for the entire kingdom to see."

"Why would I be without clothes in the garden?"

He glanced up at me from beneath his dark lashes, a smile playing on lips I knew as intimately as my own. "You mean to tell me I'm the only one who has fantasies involving that striped picnic blanket?"

The two of us. In the gardens. On the picnic blanket? "Now that you mention it . . ."

Groaning, Caiman stood and pressed a hard kiss to my temple. "If you don't stop giving me that look, we are sure to be very late."

Right. Council. Potential war.

I pressed a hand to my sinking stomach, giving myself a final once-over in the gilt-framed mirror. "I'm so nervous everyone will be judging me."

Caiman slipped his arms into his black coat, adjusting the collar before pulling his black hair back in its queue. "I hate to tell you this, but they've been judging you since the moment you arrived. This is simply another chance to remind them how brilliant you truly are."

I had trained for this. Spent summer days inside hunched over books on foreign policy and Vellanian law instead of out playing with my friends. Evenings spent with tutors and weekends learning how to walk, speak, and act at court.

Caiman's long strides carried him across the room to

where our gold crowns waited on matching velvet displays. He withdrew my crown and set it on my unbound hair. I felt its weight—the weight of a kingdom—in my soul.

You are ready.

My husband scowled down at his own crown. "It was never supposed to be mine."

"But it *is* yours." I lifted the crown and placed it where it belonged, on his head. "You deserve to wear this crown."

When he withdrew his gloves from his coat pocket, I caught his fingers, bringing his scarred hands to my lips. "Don't hide them anymore. These scars are a reminder of all you've endured in order to become the man you are today. They are beautiful."

Although he didn't appear convinced, when we left the room, the gloves remained on the unmade bed.

By the time we made it to the council chambers, the other counsellors were already seated. The moment we set foot inside, they shot to their feet. I'd expected frowns and trepidation, but all I saw were smiles from the men who would assist us in ruling this country.

Caiman beamed, withdrawing the empty chair to the right of his throne at the table's head. I thanked him, easing onto the wooden seat. Across from me, Kerrington's eyes narrowed.

"Before we begin," Caiman said, settling onto his seat, "I would like to welcome the newest member of the council, my wife and Vellana's queen, her royal highness Queen Roisin Newland Howard."

Riotous cheers and roaring applause beat in time with my pounding heart. Everyone appeared genuinely happy to have me, a fae—a woman—join their ranks. Everyone except Lord Kerrington. His icy glare left my palms damp. I scrubbed them against my skirt, determined not to let him unsettle me. I deserved a place at this table. It may take some time, but I would prove it to him and anyone else who doubted it.

Caiman must've noticed my discomfort. His smile slipped as he directed a scowl at the young Lord. "Is there a problem, Kerrington?"

"You make me sick."

Lord Devon reached for his son's arm. Kerrington jerked free, his chair scraping the tiles. "Wearing a crown that doesn't belong to you. Sitting on a stolen throne. Sleeping with your brother's wife."

My pulse thrummed in my ears.

Kerrington shot to his feet, his leg colliding with the table, rattling the ink wells on top. "Do you have any idea what your traitorous king has done?"

"Son, please," Lord Devon begged.

"It's his fault Alrec is dead." Kerrington leveled a shaking finger at Caiman. "It's all his bloody fault! And you're all just sitting here as if nothing is amiss. As if your true king wasn't murdered by this bloody traitor!"

Caiman's new guard caught Kerrington by the arm, dragging him toward the door. "You forget that I was your brother's closest mate," he bellowed. "He told me everything you did! How you forced him to go to Southbay. How you said to start the war!"

The color leeched from Caiman's face, making his wide eyes seem darker.

"That's not true," I insisted. It couldn't be true. Could it?

Caiman said nothing to defend himself. Why wasn't he

denying it? Setting the record straight for all the men gaping toward the throne?

I clutched my husband's arm. "Caiman, tell them it's not true."

His shoulders fell, and he withdrew from my grasp. "Alrec and I argued after the council meeting, the day after our father fell ill. I said he was a coward for sending his people off to fight in a war that could be avoided while he hid in the castle. He . . ." Caiman scrubbed a hand down his ashen face. "He took it as a challenge."

Lord Devon and the other counsellors started speaking all at once, each one throwing around questions, muttering curses. All I could do was stare at the man I'd married, a man so full of hate that he would goad his own brother into going to war.

I shoved away from the table and stumbled out of the room, colliding with a manservant holding a tea service tray in the hallway. The tray and teacups flew through the air, shattering on the marble tiles. I kept running from the lies, searching for safety and silence.

If Caiman hadn't fought with Alrec, he would still be alive.

I would be married to him.

Why hadn't he told me?

Why hadn't he trusted me?

By the time I reached our chambers, I still couldn't catch my breath. The unmade bed we'd shared mocked me as a fool.

"Roisin?" The door opened, and Caiman was there, hesitating at the threshold. "May I come in?"

"You are the king now. You may do whatever you like."

"Please, allow me explain."

"What's there to explain? You knew what he was like—

that he was too proud for his own good and would never back down from a challenge. And he went off to spite you and got himself killed."

Alrec had been a grown man capable of making his own decisions, a man raised to be king. He should've known better than to go marching off to war simply because of some argument. As much as I wanted to blame Caiman for that, I knew I couldn't.

"Roisin—"

"All anyone on this island has done is lie to me. I thought you were different."

"Roisin, please," he reached for my hand.

I jerked out of his grasp. *"Don't touch me."* It may not have been his fault that Alrec was gone, but it was his fault he'd never told me the truth.

"I hated my brother with every fiber of my being. But, as much as I hated him, I wish I'd bitten my tongue and kept my mouth shut. I live with my guilt every single day, eating away at me like acid." His voice broke. Tears spilled from his dark eyes. "I can't help wondering . . . I wonder if my father's death is my fault too. If he would have pulled through if his beloved son had lived. If he'd given up that bit quicker because of it."

"Alrec's death is not your fault. And neither is your father's. But this." I gestured between us. "Making the decision to keep this from me—to *lie* to me—is."

Our entire relationship had been built on a foundation of deceit.

And I wasn't sure I had it in my heart to forgive him.

22

CAIMAN

One Month Later

I woke in an empty bed. Padded through an empty room. Caught my empty expression in the mirror. All the emptiness in my life was nothing compared to the emptiness in my heart.

That's what lies did. They left you empty.

If only I had learned that lesson before it was too late.

I took my breakfast alone in my room, the same way I had every day since Kerrington had exposed my treachery to the council. Lord Devon and the rest of the counsellors had assured me that, while my actions had not been advisable, Alrec's death was of his own making.

If only I could agree with them.

When I finished my poached eggs and toast, I grabbed the same black coat I'd worn for the last three days and started for the door, where my newest guard waited with his back to the wall. He was the third man to fill the position this month. If he didn't stop huffing and puffing like he was trying to blow the walls down, he'd get the boot as well. By the time I reached the council chambers, I'd had enough.

When a tall man stepped from the alcove outside the chamber doors, my lips formed their first genuine smile in a month. "Broderick. You're back early." He'd written that he would return to Vellana by the end of the month, but I hadn't anticipated him being back so soon. "I like the beard. It suits." I scrubbed my own smooth chin self-consciously.

Broderick dipped his head, his hair a touch longer than he usually wore it. "Thank you, your highness. How goes all at the castle?"

I opened my mouth to respond, but then Roisin sauntered into view, and words failed me.

Her turquoise skirts swayed when she walked. The way she'd fashioned her silver hair into a knot at her nape showcased her long, slender neck. And the strand of diamonds from Alrec that she hadn't taken off for weeks.

"Broderick," she greeted with a wide smile. "It is good to see you looking so well."

Broderick glanced between the two of us, brow pinching. "And you, my queen." He bowed over her offered hand, kissing her fingers. She no longer wore the gold band I'd given her on our wedding day.

Roisin continued past me, into the council chambers, leaving me with a pang of longing as deep as the Vellanian sea.

My former guard gave me a pointed look.

"Later," I told him. If I was to explain all my failings, I'd need to do it over a drink. "What news from the Black City?"

He showed me a sealed letter in his breast pocket. "King Tarren desires peace and has signed the treaty."

"That quickly?" I'd heard their dealings had gone well, but no one said Tarren had actually signed the bloomin' thing. I should've been happier. "Did you learn the truth of why his ships were in our bay?"

"He claimed they were searching for a ship with black sails, captained by a pirate who stole something of great value."

He'd sent that many ships out to comb open waters? The object must have been extremely valuable. "Did he say what was stolen?"

"I asked, but he remained close-lipped."

What could it possibly be? I started for the chamber, theories flooding my mind, distracting me from ever-present misery. Today we would be voting on Roisin's charity. A mere formality, since every council member was enamored with her and her brilliant ideas for supporting the poor in Vellana City. "Have lunch with me after the meeting. You can tell me more about this mysterious—"

My words evaporated when I stepped across the threshold and found Lord Kerrington holding a blade to Roisin's throat.

Empty wine bottles had been discarded on the table and floor. The stench of stale drink made my eyes water. Behind me, Broderick cursed and reached for his weapon.

"Don't even think about it," Kerrington slurred, adjusting his grip on the dagger. Roisin whimpered, a drop of blood dribbling down her neck toward the glittering diamonds.

"Let me go," she begged.

"Quiet, fae whore!"

I held out my useless, empty hands, racking my brain for some way to save her. "Put the blade down, Kerrington. We can discuss whatever is bothering you like gentlemen."

"What's there to discuss? You stole everything from him. Everything! And now I'm stealing everything from you."

Kerrington jerked her head back by her hair. Roisin cried out and I managed a step forward before Kerrington's wild green gaze froze me in place. "Come a step closer, and I'll slice her pretty neck."

I didn't dare move again.

Roisin's sparkling silver eyes held a thousand silent pleas. "Kerrington—"

He yanked her hair harder. Another drop of blood spilled toward her necklace.

"We always knew how jealous you were," he snarled. "Saw the way you watched this one, stalking her from the shadows. And you." His cheek pressed against Roisin's. She winced, her face as pale as the marble beneath her feet. "Just another fickle fae. Who will you sleep with next? What about him?" Kerrington nodded at Broderick. "Maybe you already have. Huh?"

"Please, let her go." I would get on my knees and beg, give him anything he wanted, so long as he let her live.

Heavy footfalls pounded from down the hall. If Kerrington saw what was coming for him, he could snap. "Don't let them in," I whispered to Broderick.

Cursing, he backed toward the door, leaving me alone with Kerrington and my wife.

"The true king died, and no one cares!" He kicked one of the empty bottles, shattering it against the wall.

"I care," I told him.

"Liar!"

"Alrec would've made a brilliant king. He was strong and courageous, beloved by those around him—all things that I am not. And he loved the woman you're threatening."

Kerrington went unnaturally still.

"She loved him too," I said.

Kerrington shook his head, his unkempt red hair flopping over one eye. "She betrayed him, just as you did."

"Roisin never betrayed him. You see the necklace she's wearing? It was a gift from Alrec. And the gold slippers on her feet? Another gift. Even the dress," I said, not knowing if it was true. "She wears them because she loved him too, and she wants to keep his memory alive just like you do. He loved her more than he loved anyone else. And he would never forgive you if you hurt her." That much I could say with complete confidence. "Your quarrel is not with Roisin. It's with me."

The blade in Kerrington's hand trembled. "My quarrel *is* with you," he mumbled, shoving her aside. Roisin stumbled over her skirts, falling to the ground with a cry when her hands met shards of glass.

Before I could reach her, Kerrington lunged with his blade. Pain exploded in my chest. His bloodshot green eyes narrowed, and he whispered, "And it ends now."

I stumbled back, the hilt of a dagger stuck between my ribs and red blossoming over my white shirt. Roisin screamed, but I was already falling, my head slamming against unforgiving tiles and vicious glass. Blackness burst at the edge of my vision. I heard the sounds of a skirmish, but I couldn't move to see who had won. I tried to breathe past the pain, but it felt as if I was swallowing water. Drowning on dry land.

The most beautiful woman I'd ever seen leaned over me, her silver hair haloed by sunlight. "Stay with me," she begged. "I will never forgive you if you leave."

My biggest regret was that I would never get to tell her how much I loved her.

Death's icy fingers encircled my throat, dragging me into nothingness.

One final thought crossed my mind before my eyes closed forever:

At least I'm not alone.

23

ROISIN

A JAGGED WOUND THE SIZE OF MY HAND GUSHED BLOOD from the base of Caiman's ribs. Heat swelled along my neck as my magic insisted on healing the superficial wounds inflicted by Kerrington's blade.

"Stay with me," I pleaded, pressing my hands to Caiman's abdomen. "I will never forgive you if you leave."

Kerrington's limp body lay in a pool of his own blood. Broderick's sword clattered to the ground when he fell to my side, begging me to save the king. I closed my eyes, trying to drown out the sound of Caiman's gurgling breaths, but my stubborn magic refused to go to him.

Come on. Come on! Please. Please. COME ON.

I'd been so miserable without him, missing his presence every moment of every day. But I'd needed time to work through everything. My grief. His betrayal. My guilt. I'd taken too long. And if I couldn't get my magic to work, I wouldn't be able to save him—

Warmth spread from my chest, down my arms to where Caiman's blood soaked my fingers and . . .

Blocked.

My eyes flew open to find Caiman's closed. His chest no longer rose. I shouted for him, but he didn't wake. I tried to force my magic past the block. It refused to budge. "No . . . You can't leave me." The tears blurring my vision fell onto his blood-soaked shirt.

If only my mother were here. She was stronger. She could save him.

My mother.

Her words came back as if she'd been standing next to me.

If you could manage to force your magic past the block . . .

I had to save him.

He lied to you.

It didn't matter. Not anymore.

It would drain you of your immortal life . . .

What good was forever without the man I loved?

Despite everything that had happened, I had fallen in love with Caiman. His thoughtfulness. His quiet strength. His brazen teasing. His smiles. His taste. His touch.

"I forgive you," I said, driving my magic toward the barrier with every ounce of strength I possessed. "Please, come back. Please. *I forgive you.*"

Let me save him.

I felt the barrier bend.

I'll never ask for anything else.

Then crack.

Please. Please . . .

The barrier between us shattered, pulling me into an endless void, taking and taking until I had nothing left, and still I forced the energy from my body to his. I gave until my breaths sawed in and out and the world around me grew dark.

I would've chosen you, I shouted into the void, praying he could hear me. *If I'd known the truth, I would've chosen you.*

In the distance, a man's voice called my name. My eyes flashed open, my heart fit to burst when I felt a warm hand clasp mine and I found . . .

My hand in Broderick's.

Caiman remained still at my side.

"It didn't work . . ." It should've worked. I'd given him everything I had—everything I was—and it hadn't been enough.

"Take it," Broderick insisted, squeezing my hand tighter.

I felt it then, the buzz of magic in his palm.

"Quickly," he urged.

I quieted the questions swirling in my mind, screwed my eyes closed, and syphoned Broderick's magic. There were footsteps in the distance. Another rush of power coursed through my body. And another. And another. I directed every last drop toward the man I loved.

When I opened my eyes again, I found two more soldiers and two counsellors kneeling behind Broderick, grasping one another's hands. I recognized their faces, but their features appeared sharper. And their ears were all pointed.

Broderick let go, falling forward with a gasp.

A pair of onyx eyes blinked up at me.

It worked! I crushed my body to Caiman's, beginning to tremble. "You're alive." Caiman was alive and the color had returned to his cheeks and . . . "I thought you were dead."

"I soon will be if you don't loosen your grip," he wheezed.

I reluctantly let him go to check the pulse at his throat, thrumming steady and strong.

It worked.

Then I searched for the heat of magic that had always lived within me only to find myself utterly depleted. Not so much as a spark remained and I knew in my heart it would never return. My magic—my immortality—in exchange for his life.

A small price to pay for another chance.

Caiman's gaze darted to Broderick. "What's wrong with your . . . ?" His eyes widened. "Good heavens, man. Your ears."

A smile played on Broderick's lips. "A glamour, your highness."

"You're *fae?*" Caiman scanned the rest of the men kneeling at his side. "*All* of you?"

Broderick nodded. "I hope you can forgive the deception. We wanted to be sure of the alliance before we revealed ourselves."

"There are more of you?" I asked.

"Many, many more."

Tears spilled from between my lashes. I wasn't alone after all.

Caiman laced his fingers with mine.

I had never been alone.

"I know I lied to you," he rasped, brushing my hair from my sticky cheeks with bloodstained fingers. "But I swear, if you can find it in your heart to forgive me . . ."

"I forgive you."

His throat bobbed. A line of silver tears appeared along his thick lashes. "You do?"

"Only if you forgive me for not telling you sooner how much I love you."

Caiman's lips lifted in a tired smile as I lowered my forehead to his. "I love you too, Roisin. I always have."

My husband's love washed away the last of my

heartache. I loved him, and he loved me, and together, we would do great things.

Caiman and I may not have been married by choice.

But I liked to think we'd been married by fate.

EPILOGUE

Lady Roisin Newland loved King Caiman, second son of King Bedwyr of Vellana.

And she was proud to be his queen.

King Caiman, second son of King Bedwyr of Vellana, loved Lady Roisin Newland.

And he was proud to call her his wife.

ACKNOWLEDGMENTS

First, I want to thank you, dear reader, for picking up this book. Without you, these stories would still be sitting unread on my laptop and I'd probably be bored to tears with all the time I have on my hands.

I'd like to thank all my fellow authors in the *Arranged Marriages of the Fae* series for being so amazing. This project has been one of my favorite to date. A special shout-out to Angela Ford for building a beautiful website, organizing pre-orders, and everything else you've done to help make this series a success.

I'd also like to thank my editor Meg Dailey for fitting me into her crazy schedule and making sure these characters had silly things like goals and motivations.

My cover designer, Fran, you continue to astound me with your beautiful designs. Thank you for lending your amazing talent to this project.

Finally, to my family, I couldn't have done any of this if you hadn't left me alone. Thanks for letting me write when I needed to—and for dragging me away from the computer when I needed a break.

ABOUT THE AUTHOR

Jenny is the founder of the PANdom and a lover of books with happily-ever-afters. A native of Oakland, Maryland, she currently resides in County Tipperary, Ireland with her husband and two children. As much as she loves writing stories, she hates writing biographies. So consider this the "filler" portion where she adds words to make the paragraph look longer.

ALSO BY JENNY

The Myths of Airren

(NA Fantasy Romance)

A Cursed Kiss

A Cursed Heart

A Cursed Love (2023)

Prince of Seduction

Prince of Deception (2023)

YA Fantasy Romance

Married by Fate

The PAN Trilogy

(YA Sci-Fi Romance with a Peter Pan Twist)

The PAN

The HOOK

The CROC

Omnibus Editions

The Complete PAN Trilogy YA Omnibus

The PAN Trilogy (Special Edition Omnibus)

ABOUT THE SERIES

Arranged Marriages of the Fae is a multi-author series of short novels written by seven romantic fantasy authors on the same theme. These books can be read on their own, but you'll have so much more fun if you read the whole series!

As authors, we want to thank you for getting swept away by our fantasy romances and we wish you hours of enjoyment and escape!

XOXO

***

Married by Wind

Married by Fate

Married by Scandal

Married by War

Married by Treachery

Married by Starfall

Married by Dusk

FIND THEM ALL HERE

***

Or, choose your next read by trope!

second chance
secret identities
enemies to lovers
MARRIED BY WIND
ANGELA J. FORD
MARRIED BY TREACHERY
BARBARA KLOSS
MARRIED BY FATE
JENNY HICKMAN
MARRIED BY SCANDAL
TESSONIA ODETTE
MARRIED BY DUSK
BRIANNE WIK
MARRIED BY STARFALL
MEG COWLEY
MARRIED BY WAR
SARAH K. L. WILSON
fake dating
touch her you die
only one bed
forbidden love